LOUD MOUTH

LOUD MOUTH

AVERY FLYNN

This book is a work of fiction. Names, characters, places, and incidents are the product of the author's imagination or are used fictitiously. Any resemblance to actual events, locales, or persons, living or dead, is coincidental.

Copyright © 2020 by Avery Flynn. All rights reserved, including the right to reproduce, distribute, or transmit in any form or by any means. For information regarding subsidiary rights, please contact the Publisher.

Entangled Publishing, LLC
10940 S Parker Rd
Suite 327
Parker, CO 80134
rights@entangledpublishing.com

Amara is an imprint of Entangled Publishing, LLC.

Edited by Liz Pelletier
Cover illustration by Elizabeth Turner Stokes

Manufactured in the United States of America

First Edition June 2020

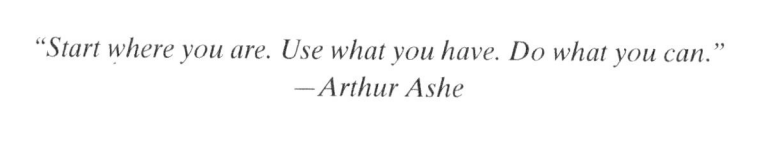

"Start where you are. Use what you have. Do what you can."
—Arthur Ashe

Chapter One

Shelby Blanton was never going to sleep again.

She should have known better than to watch a double feature about possessed houses while staying alone in a rented cabin out in the middle of snowdrift-covered nowhere.

Yeah, that had definitely been mistake number one.

The other big, bad move on her part had been that after-dinner espresso. She was a green tea drinker, but the cabin came with an espresso maker and it had totally seemed fancy and fun at the time but oh my God... She could practically hear her heart beating now and her eyes were all, *Blinking? It's for the weak!*

So now here she was, starfished on a king-size bed, practically vibrating from caffeine and wondering if every creak and groan of the cabin in the dark was actually a malevolent force waiting for her to fall asleep so it could steal her soul. The *tick, tick* had to be the huge grandfather clock—complete with antlers—in the living room. The intermittent hum was the heat kicking on and off. The shuffle of steps had to be—

Shelby jackknifed into a sitting position, one corner of the thick down comforter clutched to her chest, and told herself it wasn't an ax murderer.

Steps? It was her imagination. Or the wind. Or the pipes. Or—

Holy fuckballs, there it is again.

The noise was coming from downstairs. All of a sudden, the back-to-nature thrill of being in a cell phone dead zone without a landline became a cold blanket of dread that covered her from her chin to the little hairs on her toes. Focus glued to the bedroom door that was open—of course—she reached over to her purse on the nightstand and fished around in it until her fingers brushed by the cool metal of her flashlight stun gun. It wasn't a rock salt safety circle and a blowtorch, but it would at least give her a running start as long as the intruder was human and not a one-eyed ghoul with a grudge.

Okay, she knew the whole haunted thing was just in her head, but tell that to the lizard part of her brain that was doing the ultimate freak-out right now. That was it. She was never watching another scary movie again. Ever.

Slipping out of the bed, stun gun in her tight grip, she held her breath, straining to hear something over the sound of blood rushing in her ears as she tiptoed to the door. Taking up a spot just to the left of the open door, she flattened her back against the wall.

One of the stairs creaked and then another as someone who sounded very un-ghostlike let out a long sigh that under other circumstances would have sounded tired as hell, but considering it was made by a house-burglar-serial-killer, she wasn't about to give him any sympathy.

A nervous giggle started working its way up from her belly. Gritting her teeth, Shelby tightened her abs, hoping to stave off the very inopportune timing of her most hated reflex.

Fuck.

This was not the time for making noise—especially not the high-pitched sound that had resulted in her having the nickname The Squeaker growing up. Okay, it hadn't just been the giggle. She'd never gotten rid of her little-girl voice—no matter how many voice lessons she'd had. Now it was *that* sound that had telemarketers asking if her mommy was home when she answered the phone that was going to get her straight-up murdered.

Focus, Shelby. Be the badass your tats promise you are.

She had several, but her biggest was a detailed leaf tattoo the length of her forearm. It wasn't exactly skull-and-crossbones-with-a-bloody-dagger tough, but getting it had hurt like a bitch and she'd survived. That meant she could live through this.

The steps got closer, and she pictured a Goliath of a guy, maybe with a little drool stuck to the corner of his mouth and wild black eyes, walking toward the open bedroom door. She adjusted her sweat-slick grip on the flashlight stun gun—*thank you, nerves, for adding that to the mix*. Letting out a deep breath, she put her thumb on the switch that would turn on the super-bright light and her finger on the button that would turn on the arc of electricity.

She'd gotten the device after the threats sent in to her hockey blog The Biscuit got more than the usual you're-a-real-bitch-and-I-hope-you-get-raped variety of being female on the internet. According to the self-defense course she'd taken, the light would momentarily startle her attacker so she could get in close enough to jab the electric arc into a sensitive spot. The jolt wouldn't be enough to knock him out, but it would incapacitate him long enough for her to run down the stairs, grab her car keys, and get the hell out of this Stephen King book in the making.

The steps got closer.

Shelby forgot how to breathe.

A man walked through the door, pausing just inside, presumably looking at the tumbled-up sheets and blankets on the empty bed.

A spike of hot adrenaline stabbed the icy panic right through the heart. *Too bad, asshole, I'm not waiting for you to attack.*

Shelby let out a banshee shriek—okay, squeak. The man whirled around, hands curled into fists. She flipped on the flashlight on the inhale as he reared back, and then she shoved the arcing end into his stomach. Technically, she was supposed to hold it there for three seconds. She got maybe half of one before her grip slipped and she lost contact. He stumbled back, letting out a low rumbly yowl of pain.

That's when she was supposed to run, sprinting away from death and danger. But she didn't, not once her flashlight's beam landed on the man's face and her stomach dropped down to the cabin's wine cellar. She recognized him immediately.

Ian Petrov. Hockey player. Curly-haired, bearded sex god, according to the tabloids. Also…the one person who hated her more than anyone else in the world.

"What the hell," Ian yelled, holding a protective arm over his gut as he advanced toward her. "You better get the fuck out of here before the cops show up."

"Did you follow me?" Brilliant question? No, but her brain was a little shell-shocked at the moment.

"Why in the hell would I do th—" The word died on his lips as recognition and something that looked a lot like disgust crossed his way-too-ruggedly-handsome face. He stopped walking and groaned, letting his head drop back as he mumbled curses at the ceiling. "You have got to be fucking kidding me. You? Here? What, are you stalking me? Haven't you fucked up my life enough?"

Shelby winced. It had been an accident, but the result was the same. *She* was the reason why everyone in Harbor City now knew that Ian's best friend and fellow Ice Knights hockey player, Alex Christensen, was actually Ian's secret half brother.

When it came out that Alex had known the truth for years without telling Ian, the two men had stopped speaking to each other. Now the Ice Knights had been torn in two just as the playoffs were starting. It was an unmitigated mess. And all her fault.

Ian may not be a friendly neighborhood murderer, but he might just kill her—metaphorically. All the same, it still looked like he wouldn't mind tossing her out into the snow and leaving her to freeze in the night—and part of her couldn't even blame him.

...

Ian had been in some weird situations with women before.

There was the date who showed up in head-to-toe Ice Knights gear and asked if he wanted to see the tattoo of his face on her ass. He'd declined.

One woman had pledged daily blow jobs in exchange for helping her hook up with stern brunch daddy Coach Peppers. Ian still had no idea what a stern brunch daddy was, but if it was a guy who walked around the locker room drinking coffee that was more sugar and milk than caffeine, the team coach would qualify.

His favorite, though, was Clarissa, who had brought both her parents and her little sister along on their date. He'd had a blast at the amusement park with them, but a second date hadn't been a priority for either of them.

Never—not one single time—though, had he ever been stun-gunned in his rented Airbnb by the woman who'd ruined his life with her big mouth and who'd managed not just to figure out where he was staying for the next two weeks but to get there early.

He had to admit that before he'd Googled her, he'd never pictured the woman behind Harbor City's favorite hockey blog, The Biscuit, to have a Jessica Jones tough-chick look, but now it was made all the more jarring by the death grip she had on that stun gun of hers.

"I'm calling the cops," he said, turning on the lamp by the bed.

"To turn yourself in?" She crossed her arms and snorted in disbelief. "Perfect."

Shelby Blanton—yeah, he'd made it a point to find out her name after what she'd done—was deranged. Sure, she was hot, but definitely one crazy bitch if she thought showing up at his rental cabin was the way to get an exclusive interview or to make an apology for what she'd done. She was going to have to figure out how to increase her clout another way.

Standing his ground, he did a quick appraisal. Her dark hair was short and wavy, with one side of her scalp shaved down to such a short length, it would have made a marine recruit envious. She couldn't be more than five foot six, but even in her one-piece black thermal underwear, she managed to look tough. Maybe it was the tattoos or the nose ring—wait, it was definitely the eyes, big and dark and all but shooting laser beams of fury at him.

"Why would I call the cops on myself?" Ian asked, rubbing his abs that ached from the quick jolt from her stun gun. Fuck, he was wearing a leather jacket and a thick sweater, and it still hurt like hell. If she'd actually managed to get him for longer, his ass would be down on the ground. He probably would have pissed himself just to add to the humiliation of being held at stun-gunpoint in his own rental.

"This is my cabin," she said.

"Nice try, but I have a signed contract for this place." Check and mate.

"Big whoop, so do I, but mine is legit."

He reached for his phone and she leveled that mean little flashlight-on-steroids at him again.

His gut tensed, which made his stomach hurt even more, and he held up a hand. "Whoa, I'm already nursing an injury—don't shoot me with that thing again."

Once Shelby gave him a curt nod, he pulled his phone out and brought up the email confirmation of the booking.

"See?" He turned the phone so the screen faced his attacker.

She rolled her eyes but eventually looked at it. He doubted it was an accident that she kept her stun gun at the ready even as she stayed out of arm's reach. If it wasn't for the fact that she'd showed up uninvited *and armed* at his cabin when all he'd wanted was to be alone and drink a bottle of scotch, he might have been attracted. He wasn't going to think about that now, though.

Nor would he be dwelling on his asshole dad with a wandering dick and his *former* best friend who'd spent years lying to him. Or contemplating how several of his teammates didn't see what the big deal was. Or bemoaning the fact that he was off the ice for two weeks because he'd fallen over his own damn feet at a team dinner, gone down like a klutz without any athletic ability, and had messed up his thumb enough to need surgery. Or stewing over the seemingly never-ending media coverage of the shoving match he and Christensen had gotten into and the fact that things were hostile in the locker room, to say the least. Basically, he had a lot of things that he would *not* be thinking about while getting blasted in the cabin Lucy had rented for him to lay low while the Harbor City sports press found other things to cover.

"This is bullshit," the woman declared, but she lowered

her stun gun. "I have the same confirmation." She stomped past him to the nightstand and picked up her phone. A quick scroll later, she shoved it in his face. "See?"

A fast scan confirmed it was an exact copy of his confirmation from the rental management company for the cabin. "How'd you get this?"

"A sort-of friend arranged it for me." She tossed her phone onto the bed but held on to the stun gun even though it was loose in her grip. "Who pranked you with this confirmation?"

"One, it's not a prank." The only person he knew who would find this kind of joke hilarious was Christensen, and they might share half their DNA but that was it. They weren't friends anymore, let alone the kind who would set up something like this. "Two, it was our team PR person, Lucy—"

"Kavanagh," she finished for him.

No. Lucy wouldn't. Okay, she might have helped set up his teammate Stuckey and his now-live-in girlfriend, Zara, plus Ice Knight right winger Phillips and Tess had met and hooked up at Lucy's wedding, but she wouldn't do something like this—not with him, not now, and definitely not with Shelby Blanton. It had to be a mistake.

"Just look at this." She grabbed her phone off the bed and brought up the email that had accompanied her confirmation, and there it was in black and white.

Shelby,

I know just the place. Peaceful with gorgeous views. It's already booked. Plenty of space because the cabin is huge so you can have as much "me time" as you need without being totally alone, which you really don't want to do, considering the threats. It's just what you need. This is actually perfect.

Lucy

So much for not messing with a man when he was down. "She did this on purpose."

Shelby paled. "Why would she do that?"

"Have you met Lucy?" He shook his head, trying to wrap his brain around this mess. "She's all about controlling the situation and the spin. No doubt she thinks this will fix things."

"I can't stay here." Shelby backpedaled a few steps, clutching her phone and the stun gun to her chest.

Ian didn't need to look at his phone to confirm that it was way too late for that. When he'd pulled off the highway and onto the mile-long dirt road to the cabin with the only landmark letting him know he was on the right road being a beat-up wooden marker with the number six on it, the guy on the local radio had just announced it was ten o'clock and warned everyone to get home before the snow got any worse. Anyway, the cabin was miles away from anything even slightly resembling a town.

"Yeah, good luck with that. It's already snowing sideways out there," he said, because he had enough shit to deal with without worrying about her stuck in a snowbank because he'd kicked her out. "You can have this room. We'll figure it out in the morning."

Shelby screwed up her mouth and glared at him as if he controlled the weather or the Ice Knights' PR queen, Lucy Kavanagh. Finally, she let out a very unhappy huff. "Fine."

Okay, one battle won. He'd take it. God knew he needed it.

He started toward the door, giving her—and her stun gun—a wide birth. "Hope you don't talk in your sleep. I'd hate for you to go spilling any more life-ruining secrets."

He could have sworn he heard her mumble something along the lines of "fuck you, asshole, it was an accident" as she slammed the door shut in his face. He definitely heard the lock being turned. He couldn't blame her. The whole situation was a mess. First thing tomorrow, he'd find another cabin to sit and drink scotch in and growl at anyone who dared to cross his path. Hell, he'd rather go find a frozen hedge maze to wander until he turned into an icicle than to stay here with her.

Glancing at the window, he saw the snow piling up fast on the drive. As long as it stopped by dawn, he'd be out of here before breakfast.

...

It was a great plan, and when he woke up the next morning to bright sunshine spilling in through the huge window looking out onto the front drive, he let out a contented sigh. This was what he'd wanted, fucking serenity. Then he made the mistake of getting up from bed, walking over to the window, and glancing out.

There wasn't a driveway anymore.

The road back down the mountain to the highway was gone. Everything was covered in enough snow to obliterate any hope of an escape.

The unmistakable pitch of Shelby's voice forced its way past his closed door. "Have you seen all the stupid snow? Neither of us is going anywhere."

The sound jabbed him right in the eardrum and he winced.

His life was so fucked right now that he couldn't even manage to be alone so he could contemplate the dark pit of his existence while nursing a scotch and his misery. Instead, he was trapped here—with the woman who'd turned his life into a hellscape.

Things couldn't possibly get any worse.

Chapter Two

Three Weeks Earlier...

Two floors below the frozen surface where the Ice Knights battled for victory eight months out of the year, Shelby stood alone in the hallway halfway between the locker room and the coach's office, trying not to hyperventilate or throw up on the scuffed pumps she'd pulled from the back of her messy closet.

Her palms hadn't been this damp since she'd checked into rehab six years ago, and it hadn't been nerves that morning—it had been because she was still sweating out the vodka from one last monumental bender. This morning, her sobriety chip slipped easily through her fingers as she moved it like a magician doing a coin trick, sliding it from between one finger to the other as she stared at the closed door. Her future, the one she'd been working toward since she'd gotten clean, was on the other side of the unassuming gray door with the push-up bar running its width and a silver placard reading MEDIA ROOM next to it.

A good part of her wanted to turn tail and run. Not to

the nearest bar but to her laptop and the hockey-loving world she'd created there. The Biscuit wasn't just an Ice Knights fan blog that had grown into the most popular hockey site in Harbor City, it was her outlet. Some people went with exercise, some started vaping, some spent all their time trying to regain everything they'd lost to the bottle. Shelby had turned to hockey, the Harbor City Ice Knights in particular. And now she was graduating to the majors, a job with the team she loved, producing web content and independent analysis as part of the team's new social media platform that would be home to everything from podcasts to The Biscuit.

No more hustling for side gigs delivering food, making lattes, or temping in an office to pay the rent. This was everything she wanted, and she hadn't relied on old family connections to get it—even if one of her former stepdads owned the team. Well, not that she could just call him up. It wasn't like they'd even talked after the divorce more than ten years ago.

Now all she had to do was walk through that door.

She straightened her shoulders, let out the breath she'd been holding, and—didn't move a single, measly inch.

Girl. Get it together. Do not fuck this up.

She put her red chip with the Roman numerals for six in the inside pocket of her purse, zipping it closed with focused deliberation. Procrastinate? Her? *Oh my God, yes.* So when her cell buzzed and her mom's photo appeared on the screen, she didn't hesitate to answer.

"Hey, Mom," she said, ducking into the bathroom across the hall from the media room.

"You will never guess what Tina just told me," her mom said, her loud voice making it seem as if Shelby had her on speakerphone.

Knowing this was about to be an excruciatingly detailed peek into life in the Huckleberry Hills subdivision, Shelby did a quick scan to make sure all the stalls were unoccupied so no one else would be subject to the boring antics of one of Harbor City's most distant suburbs. Every lock on the floor-to-ceiling doors was turned to green for unoccupied.

"What did Tina tell you?" Shelby asked, not so much curious to know the answer as deeply grateful for the excuse to delay walking into the team media room.

Tina was her mom's neighborhood walking buddy. They were out together at six in the morning power walking and gossiping about everything from who put up their Christmas decorations extra early to who had the same strange car parked in his driveway three times a week as soon as his wife left for work. Both lived for the latest gossip.

"So you know how Tina has an older sister? Well, I never realized it before, but her sister's son, Tina's nephew," her mom added for unnecessary clarification, "plays hockey."

"Isn't that something." Since Shelby had started The Biscuit, her mom had been sure to share every tangentially related hockey connection she came across. "Does he play minors?"

"He plays for the Ice Knights. His name is Adam Christmas or Andy Crawford or—"

"Alex Christensen?" The forward was one of the best players on the team and an integral part of their efforts to lock in their first-place spot in the playoffs.

"That's it." Her mom let out a little crow of triumph. "But that's not the big news."

No doubt this was going to be about whomever Alex was currently dating—or more correctly, several of the whomevers Alex was dating.

"His dad is David Petrov, so that means—"

Yep. Mom and Tina definitely stopped at Tina's for Bellinis after their walk. "No, Mom, Ian Petrov's dad is David Petrov." The man was a hockey Hall of Famer who'd once scored eight goals in one game. He was a legend on the ice and the players who came after him still whispered his name as if the man really was a hockey god. "Ian plays on the Ice Knights, too."

"I *know*—that's what makes it so amazing." Her mom's exhausted, you-never-listen sigh took Shelby right back to being thirteen again. "Alex and Ian are brothers—well, half brothers, I guess—and now they get to play together on the same team. How sweet is that? You really should do a post about this. Very heartwarming."

"That can't be right." Surely someone on the team would have let it slip if it were. The two were basically inseparable on and off the ice. Someone would have noticed a family resemblance or connection.

"I think Tina would know who the father of her nephew is." Her mom paused, lowering her voice into her version of a whisper, which was still loud enough to be heard halfway across Target. "She has pictures of the two guys on her phone from a family Christmas they had eons ago. She was going through old pics and found one of the Alex guy and his humongous dad in the background. They were wearing matching sweaters. Tina said she remembers that Christmas, her sister was all weird about taking photos while the dad was there. She thinks that maybe the cops were after the David guy."

"Wow," Shelby said, her brain spinning out.

David Petrov hadn't been hiding from the cameras because of an outstanding warrant. It was because he had a whole other family. Ian's parents were still married up until a few years ago. And if what Tina was saying was true, then—

A flush sounded, the center stall door opened, and *Harbor City Post* columnist Maddie Peters walked out, a superior smirk on her face.

Shit. Shit. Shit.

This was big. Every media site in Harbor City would be all over it in a hot minute, and if all involved had been keeping it quiet on purpose, then having it blast out to the public now could really mess with team cohesion. That, in turn, could make their playoffs a disaster. None of that would matter to Maddie, though—the woman was all about getting the story no one else could, which was exactly what she'd been doing for twenty years in the ultracompetitive world of Harbor City media. She was a scary-ass legend in her own right, and she'd overheard everything.

Shelby gulped passed the oh-shit blocking her throat. "Mom," she said, sounding a little panicky because any hope of her new job being a success was balanced on this moment like an elephant on a beach ball. "I gotta go."

She hung up and tried to figure out her next move as Maddie washed her hands and then applied another layer of rose-gold lipstick. "Thanks for the scoop."

"I'm sure it was just the Bellinis talking." She gave her best impression of a chuckle, but there was no missing the edge of panic laced through it. "Tina's always been full of shit."

"Oh, don't worry," Maddie said as she walked over to the door and opened it. "I'll do my best to keep you out of it. Your shiny new place at the Ice Knights table will be protected."

Then she walked out, leaving Shelby alone—really this time—in the bathroom as she tried to figure out if she was hyperventilating or having a heart attack. Either way, she was in deep shit. A few years ago, the answer would have been to find the closest bar with the cheapest drinks, and she'd be lying if she didn't admit that the temptation was always there. And right now, it was humming in her ear like a song she couldn't get out of her head. Sometimes it was louder than others, but after six years, she was starting to be able to block it out—at least a little. She looked down at the leafy tattoo climbing up her arm, counted the thorns, and breathed deeply.

Exhaling one last time, Shelby started for the door. As unlikely as it was that Maddie would be able to confirm the story Tina was slinging, Shelby had an obligation to her new employer to let the PR people know that trouble was brewing.

. . .

Two Weeks Ago...

Ian walked into the team's workout facility, and it was as packed as a neighborhood gym after New Year's. Down to the last man in Ice Knights gear, they were all in this together, fighting for that edge that could make a difference as the playoffs approached. Last year, they'd been too cocky and had gone down in six games. That wasn't going to happen again. These were his boys and this was their year.

His phone buzzed in his workout pants for the fifth time since he'd walked into the building. Fucking A. There were a million things he'd rather do than talk on the phone, but whoever was on the other end was damn insistent. He walked through the workout room, heading for the locker room in the back to drop off his bag as he pulled out his phone right as the buzzing stopped. A notification that he'd missed a call from his dad appeared on the screen, but that wasn't what made him halt in his tracks. Instead, it was the notification right below the missed-call alert. This one was from the *Harbor City Post* and it made absolutely no sense.

Ice Knights Players Secret Brothers: David Petrov Confesses All

Considering David the dick was *his* dad and he didn't have any brothers—just two sisters who could make a grown man cry with a look—this was just nuts. He was gonna have to reach out to the team PR head, Lucy Kavanagh. She'd take care of it. Shaking his head, he continued on into the locker room. Even at one of the most crucial points in his career when everything was finally going right and he'd reached out beyond the journeyman limits everyone had expected of him when he'd been drafted in the seventh round, his dad took center stage.

At this point, he shouldn't be surprised.

It had always been like this. He was never just Ian Petrov. He'd always been David Petrov's son, held up to a standard that no one—with the exception of his buddy Christensen, fucking phenom—could come close to. Still, knowing his teammates, he was about to get a world of shit about his "brother," so he might as well see who it most definitely was not.

He clicked on the story, and a photo of him and his dad standing next to each other, matching crooked grins on their faces and the same waves in their dark-brown hair that both men hated. Right next to that photo was a years-old picture of Christensen that had been taken in the weeks before he'd been drafted. Unlike now, his light-brown hair was longer and wavier. He was smiling, but it was straight across, not crooked. How had he never noticed that Christensen and his dad had the same green eyes, the same butt-chin dimple, and the same nose right down to the pointed tip? Probably because he hadn't ever seen the two of them in the same room together, let alone in photos right next to each other. It was a weird coincidence, sure, definitely something to give a hungry reporter looking for a new angle to run with. No doubt the *Post* was going for clicks not truth when they'd written that headline.

He chuckled to himself and clicked out of the story, shoving his phone into his bag as he turned the corner to get to his assigned locker. Christensen was already there, early for once, sitting on the wood bench.

"Well, if it isn't my long-lost brother," Ian said, dropping his bag on the bench with a loud *thunk*. "Did you see that shit story in the *Post*? Man, you think they could have made up that we were going out or something?"

For once in his life, Christensen kept his mouth shut. Just sat there looking down. The first hint of unease creeped in, making him aware of the inside of his ears. It was always like this before a check he barely caught out of his periphery or before the puck came sailing his way. It was like his sixth sense and the common cold were unlikely twins.

"Dude." He stopped in front of Christensen. "No one is going to believe we're actually brothers."

"Ian." His best friend looked up, the muscle in his jaw working overtime. "I asked Lucy to buy me some time." Christensen rubbed the back of his neck, hard, his movements jerky. "I figured for sure she could make it happen. She always fixes everything."

A bone-deep survival instinct shoved away most of what had just come out of Christensen's mouth, as if it were radioactive. Instead, he focused on the rest, grabbing hold of it and refusing to let go.

"Petrov," he said, his voice harsh. "You always call me Petrov. You've never called me Ian."

Christensen rolled his eyes and threw up his hands. "That's what you want to focus on right now? That I'm using your first name?"

"Yeah," he said, squaring up in front of his friend—and that's all he was, a friend.

"Fine. *Petrov*," Christensen said, emphasizing the last name. "I never meant for you to find out this way. I meant to tell you, but the timing always sucked, and Dad didn't want me to, and—"

"Your dad," he interrupted, desperate to keep the facts— and they were facts—straight.

"*Our* dad," Christensen said, slow and deliberate.

No. That wasn't it. It couldn't be. Petrov refused to even

consider it. Palms slick, white noise screaming in his ears as his blood pumped through him at triple speed, and gut churning, Petrov tried to hold on to the world as he knew it. His parents were divorced, but they'd been married for decades. He had two sisters, Kayla and Ashley. His dad was the usual kind of jerk who came with the world thinking he was a hockey god and a shit father, but he wasn't a has-a-secret-family kind of asshole.

"When the chick from The Biscuit told Lucy how a reporter from the *Post* had overheard the story, I begged her for some time. I needed to tell you myself, to explain."

"Explain what?" Because it couldn't be what everyone was trying to sell. He refused to let it be.

"Your dad knocked up my mom and we're brothers," Christensen yelled, standing up and getting right in Petrov's face. "All right? Is that in simple enough terms for you? We share that asshole's DNA."

He shoved at Christensen's chest, hard enough to back him up a step. "Don't you talk about my dad like that."

"What? Like you're such a huge fan?" He crossed his arms, his mouth curled into a cruel smirk. "How many times have you said 'if the world only knew the real David Petrov'? About a billion seems right. He cheated on your mom and paid off mine to keep her mouth—and mine—shut tight."

"She's lying," Petrov said, the words flying out of his mouth fueled by a desperate need to keep his world intact, to protect his mom from the truth, and to maintain at least one illusion about the man who raised him. "She spread her legs for some hockey dick so she could blackmail him and has been keeping it up for years."

He was up against the lockers a half second later, the metal vents pressed against his cheek, the pain of it feeding into the jagged emotions fighting for dominance.

"Not a single fucking word about my mom," Christensen

said, his face red with fury and his eyes wet with tears. "Not. One."

And that's when he knew. He didn't need a DNA test or confirmation from his dad. Shit. He'd known the moment he'd seen that side-by-side picture. They'd both been sideswiped by the news, and now Dad's mess was theirs to clean up. He let out a deep breath and nodded to Christensen, who released him and took a step back. They eyed each other warily, both bruised in places neither could see.

"When did you find out?" Petrov asked.

"Middle school."

Hearing that was like skating at full speed right into the boards. They'd been practically inseparable on and off the ice for three years, and the whole time Christensen had known? Fuck, he really was their dad's kid. Manipulating and twisting things for his own benefit.

"So you must have had a good laugh when you got traded to the Ice Knights." Petrov pushed past the other man, checking him with his shoulder as he headed for the door. "Was it fun? Knowing all along?"

"I thought you knew, and then when I realized you didn't, I couldn't figure out how to explain. Dad said it would fuck things up for you if I did. So I kept my mouth shut."

"How convenient."

"Are you fucking kidding me?" Christensen all but roared as he rushed forward and blocked Petrov from leaving. "None of this has been convenient. While you were growing up with your rich-family reality, I was watching my mom work two jobs to pay for rent. You were the silver-spoon kid. You got vacations and family dinners and the old man showing you the hockey ropes. I didn't even get a last name."

It was too much to process; his circuits were overloaded. He was going to puke or explode or break down in fucking tears like he had when he was ten and his dad told him that hockey wasn't for everyone and probably wasn't for him. Petrov had to get out of here. Now.

"Get the fuck out of my way."

"No." Christensen didn't budge. "We need to talk."

"I said move." He shoved Christensen. Hard.

The other man went stumbling away. By the time Christensen stopped his backward momentum, Ian was already charging forward and ready to take the other man out. His dad had betrayed his family. His best friend had betrayed him by knowing the truth and never telling. Someone had to pay, and Christensen was right in front of him, grinning like a loon and as ready for a fight as he was.

"Petrov. Christensen," Coach yelled from the door, stopping them both in their tracks with just the timbre of his voice. "Cut this shit immediately. My office. Now."

Without waiting for a response, the coach spun around and stalked out of the locker room.

Glaring at each other the entire way, Ian and Christensen followed him back to his office. Lucy was already there, pacing the small cramped room and tearing whoever was on the other end of the phone a new asshole.

"You said forty-eight hours, Maddie. Unless I fell into a time warp, it's been twelve." She paused, listening. "We're talking basic human decency in letting me warn Petrov and Christensen this was coming. You said we'd have the opportunity to respond." She waited again, grinding her teeth. "Oh yeah? Fuck you and the *Post*. You're gonna regret this, Maddie Peters. Just you fucking wait."

She hung up and looked like she was ready to fling her phone across the room. Then Ian's gaze locked with hers and she let out a deep breath before shoving her phone into her purse. "Ian, Alex, I'm so sorry. I can't believe they ran with it so fast after overhearing it. And to cite The Biscuit as a source? Such bullshit. I thought we had time. I was *told* we had time to prep you both for this coming out. I'll figure out how to set this right."

Right? Was that even fucking possible? *No*, it sure as hell wasn't. They were so far beyond setting things right that it was't even a flicker in his old man's eyes.

Coach stood behind his desk, glaring at Christensen and Petrov. "And while she's doing that, I need to know from both of you that what I witnessed in the locker room isn't going to happen again." He yanked his chair out and sat down in it, the lack of height not doing one little thing to make him less of an imposing presence. "I can sympathize about this being a shit show, but we can't afford to have you act like it. You are professionals, and I expect you to act accordingly. Your team expects you to act accordingly, especially with the playoffs about to start." He eyeballed them both. "Can you do that?"

There wasn't a choice. He had to. His entire life he'd been in his dad's shadow, the journeyman player who went late in the draft—and rumor was he only made it then because of his last name—who'd finally come into his own. This run for the cup was his chance to prove once and for all that he deserved to be here. He refused to let his dad fuck this up for him. He'd worked too hard for that shit.

"Yeah, I can do that," he said, ignoring the man standing next to him.

Christensen nodded but kept his mouth closed.

"Good," Coach said, picking up his mug of sugar and milk with a hint of coffee. "So figure out how to make this work because it has to. Team dinner tonight. Don't be fucking late, either of you. And don't fuck anything up."

Yeah, it was a little too late for that. Everything was FUBARed into next week, and he had to win a championship despite all of it. They'd find a way to do just that, no matter what it took.

Chapter Three

Present Day...

Ian's injured thumb, with its short line of stitches from the surgery to repair the ligaments, hurt like hell, which suited his mood just fine as he glared at the massive piles of snow outside the big bay window on the south side of the kitchen. The drifts were frickin' huge. He strolled closer to the glass, warm bowl of strawberries-and-cream oatmeal in his good hand, and sat down so he could do the awkward-eating-with-his-nondominant-right-hand thing.

"You need some help?"

"I can eat breakfast by myself." Of course he bobbled his spoon just enough for a glob of oatmeal to drop back into his bowl.

She nodded at the coffeepot, filled to the brim with sweet beautiful black gold, and lifted a sharp jet-black eyebrow. He shrugged a shoulder. Whatever. As long as she left him the hell alone, then he'd be golden.

Still, he watched her out of the corner of his eye as she

poured half a cup of coffee, then filled the mug the rest of the way up with lukewarm water from the tap. She was hard to peg. Skinny without any hint of hips or tits or an ass, she was what his grandma would have called "a slip of a girl." But that face... He stared at her mid-bite, his spoon hovering in the air halfway to his mouth. She wasn't soft and pretty. She wasn't seductively beautiful. Instead, everything about her was sharp and tough, from her fuck-you half-shaved hair to her high cheekbones that looked like they could cut you as quick as the blade on his skates, but not as fast as the look in her dark-brown eyes.

Fuck. Way to get caught staring, Petrov.

He dropped his gaze and shoved the spoon into his mouth, the oatmeal burning the roof, of course. He just ground his teeth together and took it, the pain a useful reminder to keep his mouth shut and his eyes off her.

"You got something you want to say?" she asked, her tone a little too close to amusement for his taste.

"Nope." He shoved in another hot bite, relishing the burn.

"Well, I do."

Taking the risk, he glanced over her way again. She held the cheery red snowflake mug cupped between both hands, her gaze going past him to the snowy scene on the other side of the bay window. She looked completely out of place in the country winter wonderland kitchen with her ripped black jeans, oversize black sweater with its ragged edges on the sleeves, and detailed leaf tattoo climbing up her arm, visible beneath her pushed-up sleeves.

But that wasn't what made his muscles tense all the way from his toes to his shoulders. It was that she had that little bit of a lost look in her eyes that he had to steel himself against. This wasn't just a person in the kitchen—this was the woman who'd blasted his life apart.

"Haven't you already said enough?" he asked. "I realize you're just trying to build your reputation even more, maybe snag the opportunity to renegotiate your brand new contract for more money, but I'm not now nor am I ever going to open myself up in front of the world."

She closed her eyes, her jaw flexing, and let out a huff of frustration.

"Counting to ten?" he asked. "Or twenty?"

"Neither." She glared at him. "I'm reminding myself why I should bother to apologize to you."

"Oh yeah?" He snorted. "You gonna butter me up and then pump me for how I'm feeling, so you can sell that bit of information off for fun and profit?"

Wouldn't that just be the poisoned cherry on this shit sundae. Everyone wanted to know how he was *feeling*, how he was dealing with the news. Fucking angry and by getting drunk—hopefully soon—were the answers, but he sure as fuck wasn't sharing that with the world.

"You're a real jerk," Shelby said, her voice quiet and a little bit trembly.

He shrugged. "What can I say, apple doesn't fall far from the tree."

"I'm sorry."

"For my dad's wandering dick and my lying best friend? How sweet of you to share. Can we go back to absolute silence now?"

"No, I'm sorry that I was a giant chicken and took my mom's call so I wouldn't have to walk into that media room, that I didn't better check to make sure no one else was in the bathroom because my mom is a very loud talker, that when Maddie overheard my mom, I didn't have a *Men in Black* memory destroyer thing to zap her with, and, most of all, I'm sorry that this is how you found out."

He froze. Mom. Overheard. Bathroom. "What are you

talking about?"

"That's how the news got out and I'm sorry, but I had no idea what my mom was about to say or that her friend was even telling the truth."

"You didn't tell the *Post* on purpose?"

"No. Who in the hell would do that?" When he didn't answer, she looked up at the ceiling and muttered something he didn't catch. "Oh yeah, that would be me. Someone who doesn't know you beyond your playing stats but who took a deep dive into your past to find the one secret you didn't even know you had, just so I could expose it and make a name for myself." She marched over to the doorway leading out onto the porch, her voice growing louder and tinnier with each step, and shoved her feet into snow boots—black, of course—and grabbed a dark puffer coat off the hook. "Of course, I'd probably end up getting fired from my brand-new job and become a hockey pariah in the process, but you know nothing is too high a price to pay to expose you. That sounds totally legit." She shoved her arms into the coat, zipped it up, and snapped the bottom of the hood together until the only parts of her face visible were her eyes and pointy nose. "Not everyone in the world is here to screw you over, you big, mean jerk."

And with that, she stormed out of the cabin. He watched as she slip-stomped down the snow-covered steps and swiped a shovel that was leaning against the railing, his mind trying to unravel what she'd just said.

How was it suddenly his fault Shelby was the loud mouth who'd leaked to the press just because it wasn't on purpose? Who could blame him for being upset, what with the press being on his ass since he hit juniors? They loved to report about how he was good but not great like his dad—that he never would be. For years he'd fought against it. Then he'd sort of learned to accept it. The stories comparing him to his legend-on-the-ice of a father kept coming, though. Ian had come to his suspicion and loathing of the press and all media types, including places like The Biscuit and Shelby herself, honestly. These were people who lived to fuck other people over and knock them down. End of story.

This latest twist only served to prove his point. Fan comments that all the hockey talent in the family must have gone to the son who'd been picked in the first round, the one whose plus/minus average had been among the best in the league since his rookie season, the one who'd known the truth and had never said a damn word. The press loved to see someone get laid low and report all the gory details. It got clicks, that was for sure.

He took another bite of oatmeal, all the bitterness in his brain affecting the taste and turning the strawberries sour, as he watched Shelby—her hood down now—try to shovel out a subcompact. The wind pushed back her hood, whipped at her short hair, and turned the tips of her ears red. The snow went past the tops of her snow boots and nearly up to her knees as she worked to clear a path for her itty-bitty car.

How in the hell had that speck of a car managed to make it up the mountain in the first place? There was no way with all the additional snow, which was starting to come down in ever faster waves, it would be safe for her to attempt the twisty roads. He couldn't let her do that. It was too dangerous. He was up and out of his seat before he knew what in the hell he could do about the situation. Then a gust of wind strong enough to make the roof rattle blasted the mountain. The falling snow went sideways, the trees bent under the pressure, and a large limb snapped off, slicing through a power line before hitting Shelby and sending her flying back onto her ass in the snow.

He was out the door before her shocked scream sounded, racing toward her like he was on a breakaway.

• • •

One second Shelby was lost in a snowdrift, her upper arm aching, and the next she was tucked securely against Ian's chest as he carried her inside the cabin. Even with as fast as they were hustling up the steps to the porch, her being buffeted by unyielding biceps and pecs, she didn't move a millimeter.

"What are you doing?" The words were barely out of her mouth before her brain clocked how dumb they were, but Ian smelled good, like, really good, and it was distracting as hell.

Her senses must be heightened by her near brush with getting beaned by a tree limb the size of a Louisville Slugger. Why else would she be noticing that warm, spicy scent that clung to him? Or that he had a very nice chin under his dark scruff, and his eyelashes were a billion miles long? The tingly, breathy thing she had going on right now, making her chest tight, was no doubt left over from the adrenaline rush of dodging the limb mixed with the oh-shit-that's-cold jolt from landing in the snowbank. That had to be the reason why she didn't demand to be put down and instead had asked such a duh question.

"I'm helping you," he said, gaze forward, body stiff.

"Why?"

He turned sideways and used his hip to nudge the front door the rest of the way open. "Because I'm not a total dick, and you're hurt."

She lifted her arm, testing it as they crossed the threshold, passed the kitchen, and hustled straight into the living room with its ginormous stone fireplace that looked like it just might have been here centuries before the house. The clock on the microwave had gone dark, the lightbulbs in the deer-antler chandelier were off, and the heat that had been pumping out of the vents was no more. Oh shit. Any hope that the wire the limb had taken out before landing on her wasn't the power line vanished.

"I'm okay," she said under her breath, willing it to be true.

"Well, then," Ian said, unceremoniously dumped her onto the couch, and kept walking, flexing his hands as if carrying her had stung. "I'll get started on the fire."

Okay, obviously Ian did not take that the way she'd meant it. She sat up, slipped off her boots, then clutched a pillow to her chest and practiced her deep breathing. Panic attacks weren't really her thing, but neither was being trapped without power in a cabin with someone who seemed to hate her even as he rushed to her aid.

While her annoyed knight-in-ass-hugging-jeans squatted down in front of the fireplace, Shelby took off her coat and pulled her arm out of the sleeve of her sweater to get a better look at where the limb had hit. A purple bruise was already starting to bloom, but that seemed to be the worst of it.

Finally, something was going right. Really, at this point something had to land on her side of the ledger.

"Why are you getting undressed?" Ian asked, his voice gruff.

Glancing up from the monster bruise forming on her arm, she rolled her eyes at him. "I'm not."

He gestured at her bare arm.

Oh for the love of— "I'm wearing a tank top under my sweater and it's literally just my arm. Why are you being weird?"

Instead of answering, he just grunted and turned back to the fire.

Okay, Mr. Chatty.

After slipping her arm back in her sweater, she took her phone out of her coat pocket and swiped the screen. Just as she had the night before, she only had half a bar. Well, it was worth a try. She dialed Lucy's number and waited as a message reading "connecting" appeared above the keypad and stayed there. Moving the phone in hopes of catching the elusive second bar, she walked around the living room with no luck. Without giving Ian a second look—okay, much of a second look, he was wearing a Henley for God's sake and had biceps for days—she stuffed her feet into her unlaced snow boots and went out onto the porch. She got as far as the railing before the call started to ring through.

Thank you, snow fairies.

"Hi, you've reached Lu—" Static ate away the rest of Lucy's greeting. "Leave a mess—" More aural fuzz. "Call you back."

The beep came through loud and clear.

"Lucy, I'm at the cabin and Ian Petrov showed up—but you know that already. Long story but the power just went out. Our cars are buried in all this snow. If anyone can figure a way to get us out of here, it's you. And you owe us for setting this up."

In an effort to block the icy wind blowing in all directions that sent the quicker-falling snow swirling around her, she turned and ended up facing the large living room window. Ian stood on the other side, his feet planted hip-width apart and his arms crossed over his muscular chest, glaring straight at her. Again. What was with this guy? He rushes to pluck her out of the snow and carries her back to the house like something straight out of a movie but then gets sulky the moment she says her arm isn't about to fall off? Did he want to play hero or watch her writhe in pain? Falling back on the skills she learned as an angry, disaffected teenager, she itched her nose with her middle finger while scowling right back at him. Mature? Nope. Satisfying? Yes.

"If we kill each other, I'm going to come back as a ghost just to haunt you," Shelby said into her phone as she turned away from the man who totally discombobulated her. "Call back and send help, please."

Sending up a prayer that the message wouldn't be totally garbled, she squared her shoulders and walked back into the cabin. The heat from the now-crackling-to-life fire hit her as soon as she walked in the door, a welcome blast of comfort after the frigid ice fingers of the wind reaching through her sweater. It was like getting out of the shower and wrapping a fresh-from-the-dryer towel around herself.

Closing her eyes, she let out a long, satisfied sigh. When she opened them again, Ian was staring straight at her, and she would have sworn she'd caught a glimpse of something softer for a whole half a second before his body tensed and he went back to his usual lump-of-stone posture.

Okay, then.

"I left a message for Lucy," she said, taking off her boots and heading straight toward the fireplace, hands tingling in anticipation of the heat. "The connection wasn't the greatest, but hopefully enough of it got through."

He nodded and did that growly grunt of his again before stepping away from the fireplace as she approached it, his moves hurried. His heel caught on the corner of the rug. His eyes went wide with surprise and he flung his arms out for balance as he started to tip over. Shelby didn't think, she just reacted, calling up on that adrenaline-spiked quick reflexes and reached out, catching his hand and pulling him forward, helping to hold him steady as he fought to stay upright in a long, drawn-out moment that was probably all of half a breath long. Then he was stable, looking down at her, the muscle in his jaw working overtime as the air crackled around them.

"Thanks," he said, a tinge of pink hitting his cheeks. They were so close, the heat from his body rivaling what the fireplace was kicking out. "You're stronger than you look."

"Have you ever met a woman before?" she asked, mentally warning herself not to notice the flecks of green in his brown eyes or the tiny scar across the bridge of his nose or the way her pulse was kicking it up a notch or four thousand. "Of course we are. We have to be."

He ran his thumb over the back of her knuckles—soft and tentative, as if he didn't understand why he was doing it. Then he exhaled a harsh breath, lifted his thumb, and scowled at her. "You can let go now."

Shelby flinched and dropped her hand. She'd been trying to help. It wasn't like she wanted to hold his hand, or touch him, or—

I should have just let him fall on his ass. Way to go, Past Me.

"We need to shut off the other rooms and keep this fire going," he said, closing the door that led from the open-concept living/kitchen space to the hall that led to the back of the house and then heading for the stairs. "Since there aren't fireplaces upstairs and there's no way we'll get power all the way up here until after the storm's gone, we gotta shut this room off as much as possible."

Wait. What? No. That wasn't right.

"Heat rises," she said. "I'll just stay in my room upstairs under some blankets. It'll be fine."

Okay, that sounded lame even to her ears. The more open space the heat had to fill, the less there would be.

"Shelby, we don't know how long it's going to be until either help arrives or we can drive back down the mountain," Ian said as he climbed the stairs. "This is us for the next few days. Believe me, I hate it, too."

And there it was, the shit sandwich of a situation. She was trapped with Ian Petrov in a cabin without power while the snow picked up speed outside and the wind howled. Yeah, when this was all over, she was most definitely going to come back as a ghost and haunt Lucy for getting her into this mess.

Chapter Four

Why was it that the thing a person was looking for was always in the last spot they checked? Ian grabbed the cast-iron skillet from the weird half-size cabinets above the built-in microwave and brought it over to the fireplace. The sun had dipped below the mountains and he'd augmented the light from the fire with about a dozen candles he'd found in the hall closet. No one was going to mistake it for high noon, but there was definitely enough light to cook dinner without worry of slicing a finger open instead of the fat steak he'd taken from the fridge.

"What's all this?" Shelby asked as she walked down the stairs, looking like an extra from a postapocalyptic movie about badass women surviving in a new Ice Age.

She wore a long-sleeve black thermal shirt with buttons all the way down the front that weren't tempting at all, a snug pair of black thermal pants that made leggings seem like religious wear, and had the thick comforter covered in silhouettes of grizzly bears from her bed wrapped around her shoulders and flowing behind her like a cape. She clutched a pillow and a duffel bag that looked to be about the size of a small car compared to her twiggy frame and obviously was throwing her off-balance. Weighed down like she was, when she moved from one step to the next, she bobbled a bit before regaining her balance, twisting her mouth in determination and descending to the next level. The same process repeated with each step, the tension increasing and making his gut twist with dread.

He stomped over to the stairs. his gaze trained on her foot as it came within a skate's blade of missing the step. "Don't move."

Her eyes went wide with shock but she stayed in one place. "Why?"

"Because you're gonna kill yourself, and the cops will never believe that you insisted on coming down the stairs loaded down like an overwhelmed pack mule."

She grinned down at him, showing off a prominent gap between her two front teeth. "Two trips is for losers."

"And people who aren't into concussions or breaking their own damn neck," he grumbled as he hustled up the stairs, getting to her level before she managed to lose the battle with gravity and balance.

He lifted the duffel bag from her shoulder and took the pillow from her grasp, shoving it under his arm before turning and heading back down, his annoyance with himself increasing with each step. Why in the hell was he helping her? He could have been snowed in here by himself, drowning his misery in scotch and stewing in the wreckage of the life he'd thought he'd been living.

Instead, here she was, the reason for his misery—okay, to be fair she was the messenger of his misery, but every time he thought about his dad and Christensen, it was like getting whacked on the back of the head with a two-by-four. Being mad at Shelby hurt less.

He let out another harsh, angry breath.

"Are you always this surly when you're helping people?" Shelby asked, trailing behind him, all darkness except for the ridiculous comforter and her voice that sounded like she'd just taken a partial hit of helium.

"Yes."

"Then you could at least have the decency to not look all *Witcher* hot while you do it."

That stopped him cold and he turned around, glowering. "What is *Witcher* hot?"

The beginnings of an amused smile tilted the corners of her mouth upward. "Do you grunt?"

Okay, he wasn't sure where this was going, but he didn't like it. "Occasionally."

She shot him an oh-really look. "In the past twenty-four hours, you've grunted so much that I can tell the difference between their meanings. Plus, you just did it, like, five seconds ago."

He let out a huff of breath that rumbled in his chest as he dropped the duffel at the end of the oversize couch. It was a massive piece of furniture that had to have been custom-made. Roughly ten feet long, it ran the span of the living room with each end being bracketed by two chaises wide enough to be an extra-wide twin-size bed. It wasn't as good as separate rooms while he was snowed in with her, but it was better than freezing his ass off in a snowbank.

"See!" Her triumphant tinkling laugher filled the cabin.

"I did that on purpose." Not really, but he wasn't going to admit that to her. "I don't do it otherwise."

She let her head fall back and laughed as if he'd just told the world's funniest joke.

"Absolutely no one believes that. You are a grunter. A scowler. An eyebrow raiser." She waved her hand in his direction with enough enthusiasm that the comforter nearly fell off from around her shoulders. "And you like to stand with your arms crossed when you're wearing a Henley so we all know without any doubt just how big your biceps are."

"What's a Henley?" That came out of his mouth, but all that was running around his head was that she'd been checking out his muscles.

"What you're wearing. What do *you* call it?"

He looked down. "A shirt." He'd gotten the *Henley* because it was soft and comfortable. Because he hated shopping, he'd gotten twelve of them in three shades. Between these shirts, his collection of sports-related T-shirts, and a healthy collection of workout stuff, he was pretty much set when he wasn't in uniform on the ice or in one of the stupid suits Coach insisted they wear before and after games. She thought it showed off his guns, huh? He crossed his arms again, being sure to tuck his hands under his biceps to really set them off. And *bingo*, he saw it. A rusty chuckle escaped. "Never noticed that before."

"Believe me," she said, her cheeks a little pink. "Other people did."

Other people, huh? Or maybe just Shelby? Did his chest puff? Did he flex a bit? Did he start getting thoughts he didn't need to have? Yeah, he did. Sue him. "Why does it make you so mad?"

She rolled her eyes. "It doesn't."

"It sure seems to bother you." Yeah. He wasn't convinced, especially since she wasn't looking at his face. Nope. Her gaze had traveled lower. "Or maybe it's more that it gets you hot and bothered?"

Did he sound like his grandpa saying that phrase? Sure shooting (another PopPop special), but he leaned into it, enjoying feeling something other than seriously pissed off for the first time in weeks.

Her cheeks flamed. "You're obnoxious."

"And hungry." He waited a few seconds to see if her blush could darken any more. "Which is why I am about to make us dinner."

"I think I liked you grunty better." But that twitchy trying-to-fight-off-a-smile of hers was back.

"Steak," he said, figuring it was time to get back to the matter at hand. "Yes or no?"

She sighed, sending the puff of her short wavy hair up from her forehead. "Yes."

"Perfect." He walked over to the fireplace and set the metal screen down on the two bricks that had already been in the fireplace. "Maybe if you're eating, you can't spread all the secrets you've ever heard about me."

You just couldn't help yourself, could you?

This time she grunted, and it didn't take much skill to translate it as a snarly little *fuck you*, especially since when he looked over his shoulder, he caught her flipping him off. Oh God, this was almost as good as busting his teammates' chops in the locker room. It was just the sort of thing he'd been missing since all hell had broken loose—well, one of them. He'd almost forgotten what it was like to enjoy a little trash-talking fun. He wasn't about to ruin his mood by thinking about his now-dead friendship with Christensen.

Before his brain could pounce on that thought and inspect it obsessively from every possible angle until he was three seconds away from chucking out his entire hockey career to go live in the woods, Shelby let her comforter drop. He tightened his grip on the cast-iron pan before he dropped it on his toe and found himself out of the lineup even longer.

Ian had never been a guy with a type. Every woman had something about her that was sexy and intriguing and grabbed him by the balls, demanding his admiration. Seeing Shelby, though, in the soft light being thrown by the huge-ass fireplace and all the candles he'd dug up did something else.

It made his gut flop and his toes sweat just like before a big game when everything was on the line and the stakes had never been higher. It made no fucking sense. The woman had fucked up his life. That she hadn't done it on purpose didn't matter. Intent didn't eliminate responsibility.

It was going to be a long few days before a snowplow got to them.

. . .

Belly full from a perfectly cooked steak and warm baked apples, Shelby started shuffling the cards she'd found in the drawer of the wooden coffee table with a scene of deer in the meadow carved into its polished finish. Across from her, Ian was sucking down the last of the orange juice, seltzer, and one scoop of rainbow sherbet that had been her go-to treat drink since she'd gotten out of rehab. Thank God the Airbnb people had stocked the fridge and pantry. At least they wouldn't starve. Maybe it was because the hangry had abated, but they hadn't sniped at each other since dinner had started, and Ian had only grunted twice.

And with hours to go until bedtime, the books on her tablet weren't going to do her any good, since she'd forgotten to charge before the power went out. Beyond anything else, not having access to her latest read when she only had four chapters left to go and everything was chaos was pretty much the definition of sucking big-time.

"You gonna deal or just shuffle for the rest of the night?" Ian asked as he adjusted the pile of pillows he was sitting on, then adjusted them again and again.

Shelby bit down on her lower lip as she watched him be all snarly with the pillows, stifling the giggle desperate to escape. It shouldn't be funny, but it was. He was like the princess and the pea over there.

Once he finally settled, she finished shuffling and put the cards in the middle of the table. "Did you decide what game you want to play?"

For the first time since he'd marched into her room like an avenging ghost, he smiled, and it transformed his entire face and was like catching a glimpse of a happy oasis in a desert of grump. "Slap Jack."

She snorted. "Yeah right."

"What?" He crossed his arms over his chest, the uh-huh-that's-right look on his face showing that he knew exactly how good his arms looked at the moment. "It's fun and fast."

"Your thumb." She pointed at his hand. "The one that you had surgery on? The one that's the reason why you aren't playing right now even though the team needs you?"

He shrugged. "I'll use my other hand."

"That doesn't seem like the best idea."

He grunted—of course—which she most definitely wasn't beginning to find amusing. She was just getting used to it so it annoyed her less, that was all. And the butterflies bouncing around in her stomach? It had to be steak-related. Who could afford a thick, juicy piece of meat that size on her salary? And yes, she *was* talking about the steak and not the man, thank you very much.

She cut the deck in half, sliding one stack over to him and keeping one for herself. "You're going down, Petrov."

"Not gonna happen. I have professional-grade reflexes."

That might be true, but she had three-fourths of the deck within minutes. If he had been someone else, she just might be thinking that he was hesitating so he didn't smack her hand into a pancake—but this was Ian Petrov. He'd growled at her earlier today. Literally growled. Plus, if he even made eye contact with her, he was scowling half a heartbeat later. That whole don't-hate-the-messenger thing was definitely not part of his personal philosophy. So the game continued as the fire crackled and the wind howled outside. King of hearts. Two of spades. Nine of spades. Four of diamonds. Jack of—

Shelby slammed her hand down on the pile a fraction of a second too late, landing on Ian's hand with a resounding *thwack*. His eyes went wide and he sucked in a quick breath before looking down. He'd used the hand with his injured thumb.

"Oh hell, I'm sorry." She shot up from where she sat crosslegged and nearly collapsed back down as invisible pins and needles jabbed at her because she'd sat in the circulation-destroying position for so long. "Are you okay?"

"Fine," he said before he even looked down to make sure his stitches were still in place. "It was my fault." He glared at her. "I got distracted."

Okay, she wasn't exactly a fan of losing, either, but what the hell was with all the dirty looks? She hadn't meant to whack him. He was the one who used his injured hand *and* suggested Slap Jack.

"Do you need me to look at it?"

He pulled his hand close like she was going to cleanse the wound by shoving his thumb into the fire. Trust issues? This guy? Yeah, he was pretty much a wounded bear. Of course, that didn't excuse him from being an ass. Come on, they were both adults. Shitty stuff happened to everyone. Part of adulting was figuring out how to move forward without firebombing the place.

"Nah," he said, relaxing a few degrees as if he realized he'd flinched. "I'll live—and eventually the sports press will stop giving me shit for getting injured by falling over my own feet."

"Could be worse. Do you remember the goaltender who tweaked his shoulder blow-drying his hair and had to stay off the ice?"

Ian chuckled. "And then there was Ron Tugnutt—real

name—who messed up his groin when he bent over to tie his shoes."

"Or," she said, getting into the spirit of the moment, "the guy who busted up his hand cleaning his bagpipes—not a euphamism."

They were both snickering by now at the ridiculousness of it. Hockey wasn't an easy sport. It was hard checks, illegal hits, and fighting over a frozen piece of vulcanized rubber that could knock your teeth out and break bones if it hit a player right. Still, the players played through it all, even if it meant wincing on their way to the bench and spending the time between shifts trying to fight through the pain.

God knew, she'd seen it enough going to games with her former stepdad before he'd hit it big and had earned enough to finally buy the team he'd always loved.

Of course, that hadn't happened until after Jasper Dawson and her mother divorced. After that, they'd lost touch because it wasn't like they'd even been related for that long—her mom rarely made it past the year-and-a-half mark before setting her eyes on freedom. Still, when Shelby saw the news about Jasper, she'd celebrated that little victory of his from her room at the rehab clinic, telling everyone about how for one glorious season she and Jasper had season tickets right behind the bench.

It had gotten so cold down there at that level, and by the end of the games, there was no mistaking the smell of the sweat-soaked hockey pads, but it had been absolutely wonderful. So when her counselor had recommended she find a hobby that she could pour her energy into instead of pouring herself into a bottle, the Ice Knights had been it. And The Biscuit had been born out of a place of desperate hope for the future.

"So you're saying I'm in good company?" Ian asked, dragging her back to the here and now.

"Well, you're at least not alone. I'm not sure it's the same thing." She held out her hand. "Now, let me see your thumb."

He didn't move. She lifted an eyebrow, ready to go to battle.

Finally acceding, he put his hand in hers. Turning it over, she noticed the little nicks and scars dotting his knuckles, no doubt from years of playing hockey. Heart beating fast, she brushed her fingertips over the back of his hand before turning it over to get a better look at his injury. The stitches were perfectly lined up, tiny and angry-looking after that smack, but none was torn.

Good. Great. You can let go now, Shelby girl.

She could.

She didn't.

Instead, she made the mistake of looking up and catching him not glancing down at his thumb but staring directly at her with what sure as hell wasn't a thank-you-for-checking-on-my-boo-boo look. It was the kind of look that promised the best kind of dirty things and had her shifting on her pillows. There were just so many bad possibilities, the really good bad kind that involved nudity and licking and touching and orgasms for everyone and—

Oh my God, Shelby. Calm the fuck down before you embarrass yourself. He is just looking at you, not getting naked and eating you out by the light of the fire.

And that was a mental image she most definitely did not need in her head right now.

Especially since he hates your guts—and not exactly without cause.

Oh yeah, thanks for that little reminder, asshole who lives in my head.

Pulling herself back from the edge of making a complete fool of herself, Shelby let go of his hand and then sat on hers. It never hurt to be extra careful.

"Ian," she said, not having any kind of clue what should come next.

He grunted in acknowledgment and God help her, she had to squeeze her thighs together for some kind of momentary release because good dinner plus fireplace plus hot man equaled horny times to her completely unhinged id.

Focus, Shelby.

"I'm sorry about how the story of Alex being your brother got out and my part in it. I hope someday you won't hate me for it." The words came out in a rush and without even a hint of forethought because why should her nonexistent filter make an appearance now?

He sat back suddenly, as if she'd stuffed a fresh-made snowball down the back of his shirt and looked over at the fire. The muscles in his jaw flexed as he ground his teeth together before letting out a deep breath.

"Okay, so I'm just gonna turn in now," she said as she hustled over to the part of the couch were all her stuff was. "Night, Ian."

He didn't say anything as she grabbed her toiletry bag and went into the main-floor bathroom to brush her teeth. By the time she got back, he was brushing over the kitchen sink and watching the snow continue to fall outside the big bay window in the breakfast nook. He'd swapped out of his jeans and Henley for a pair of track pants.

She didn't mean to look so long at his back but damn, it was hard not to take it in. Broad shoulders topped off a muscular back that tapered down to narrow hips and a hockey butt to beat all hockey butts. The man had to get special pants made just for him. Catching herself just as he started to turn around, she dove under the covers on her side of the couch and closed her eyes so he might maybe think she was done talking and ready for sleep.

The floorboards creaked and the covers rustled at the

opposite end of the sectional, where she did not picture Ian stretched out with the blanket down at his waist. Shirtless. It really needed to stop snowing outside so she could shovel out her car and get gone.

"Hey, Shelby," Ian called out, a raspy edge to his voice.

She swallowed. "Yeah?"

"I don't hate you," he said.

Every thought in her head skittered to a stop. She would have formed words if she could have, but an apology from Mr. Sexy Grunts was pretty much the last thing she'd been expecting. Ever. Like she would go work for the hated Cajun Rage before laying even a dollar on the chance he'd say he'd been wrong about being pissed at the messenger—even an accidental one.

"Wake me up if the fire goes out." Then he rolled over, and all of fifteen seconds later, his breath had steadied and he was asleep.

Meanwhile, Shelby was left staring at the shadows from the fire flickering on the ceiling and wondering if she would ever sleep again. Verdict? Probably not until she left this cabin, because if she was that attracted to Ian when she'd figured he was mad at her, finding out that he wasn't was going to give her sexual-frustration insomnia to the twelfth degree.

Chapter Five

Ian couldn't sleep. He'd faked it long enough for Shelby to crash out, but not even the soothing crackle of the fire could help lull him under. He was too aware of her. He couldn't see a lot of her in the light of the fire, but he could see enough that his imagination could fill in all the details, which had left him with a head full of Shelby and half a hard-on.

Fuck, he needed to cool off. Since throwing himself into one of the snowdrifts outside wasn't an option unless he wanted to freeze his dick off, he got up and went into the kitchen. He grabbed one of the water bottles from the pantry and took a huge gulp as he scrolled on his phone in vain, looking for hockey updates when he didn't have shit for a signal.

It wasn't the best use of his battery, but it was better than sitting on the couch thinking about Shelby, because she was very much off-limits.

When the new owner had come in, he'd gone over in great detail how there was to be no fraternization, as he put it, between players and anyone else involved with the team.

With his busted thumb, the drama in the locker room, and the fact that the Ice Knights were in a fight for their playoff lives, the last thing Ian needed was to make more waves for the team. All he wanted was to keep his head down, do his job, and stay the fuck away from Christensen.

As long as that happened, he could finish out his contract in Harbor City and then transition into a career in coaching.

He was a man with a plan, and he was sticking with it no matter how tempting Shelby was.

Water finished, he set his phone down on the edge of the counter and then crumpled the plastic bottle before shooting it basketball-style into the recycling bin on the opposite end of the counter. During the day, the sound would hardly register, but in the middle of the night with the wind finally calmed down, it boomed in the open space. He whipped around to make sure he didn't wake Shelby, accidentally hip-checking his phone off the counter. It crashed down onto the hard tile floor, hitting just right so that his screen cracked in three places.

Fucking A.

He jerked his gaze over to Shelby on the couch, but she was still—amazingly—dead to the world. Curled up on her side, her breathing steady and the occasional mumbled word coming from her lips.

Instead of looking softer in her sleep, she managed to still look badass, even with that stupid bear-covered comforter pulled all the way up under her chin. It was her lips that really got to him, though. Full, pale pink, and slightly parted in sleep. His cock started to thicken against his thigh and he forced himself to pivot from thinking about her mouth to rehashing every missed pass he'd ever had in his career—yes, he remembered them all.

He'd been an ass to her enough as it was without adding in her waking up and spotting him sporting a tent in his pants as he watched her sleep. She'd probably go after him again with her Taser, and he wouldn't blame her.

Making his way over to the fireplace, he grabbed a couple of logs and put them on the fire, using the poker to push them in place so the blaze would continue through the night. Waking up in an icebox wasn't something he wanted to deal with. Of course, he'd have to fall asleep first. That wouldn't be an easy task even if Shelby wasn't here.

He was a man with a sleeping routine and without it, he was a man without sleep. He needed mostly quiet, total darkness, his white-noise app, and a solid hour of staring at his ceiling.

"Robber baron moose on a train," Shelby said. "Look out."

Ian jerked around. "What?"

Shelby's eyes were still closed and she was half in a ball like before. She was talking, but there was no way she was awake.

"Orgasms give you endorphins; that's what I told the conductor." She shoved her comforter down to her waist. "I love to dance, don't you?" She sat up, her eyes open but her face blank. "The moose is waiting for you."

He knew she was just talking in her sleep, but Ian still looked over his shoulder at the huge kitchen window. Just a few months ago, there'd been a story in the *Harbor City Post* about a seven-hundred-pound moose (a small one, the article had noted) that had busted into a cabin to get out of a snowstorm. It had taken a massive tranquilizer to knock it out so it could be treated for injuries from going through the glass and relocated back out in the wild. Luckily there wasn't a moose out on the porch that he could see, but still it was one more thing that his brain would be directing as he tried to get it to shut up long enough for him to go to sleep.

"This is my song." Shelby shoved more at the comforter,

as if she was going to get up. "I've never slow danced with a moose before. Don't step on my feet."

Worried she'd hurt herself, Ian rushed over to the couch and gently pushed her back down, adjusting the covers so they were back up at her chin. Then, pulling a move from his mom's playbook when he was a kid and couldn't sleep, he ran his fingers over Shelby's hair. Brushing over the prickly buzz of the close-cropped side to the silky smooth waves over and over slowed the spinning of his thoughts, and relaxing back into the couch cushions, he closed his eyes.

Suddenly, she jolted into a sitting position, completely awake, and scooted away from him, her eyes wide and not even a little bit sleepy. "Why are you petting me?"

He held up his hands, palms forward. "It's not what you think."

"You weren't petting me while I slept?"

"You started talking about a moose on a train." The words came out as fast as a slap shot. He did not want her freaked out that she was trapped with a hair-petting weirdo. "And then dancing and then you tried to get up and I thought you'd trip over the coffee table or something. I was trying to get you to go back to sleep, and the whole hair thing was one of the tricks my mom used to use on me."

"Oh God, I haven't done that in years." She let out an embarrassed groan and slumped against the couch. "Did I wake you up?"

He shook his head. "I'm not a good sleeper, and I can't without the white-noise app on my phone."

"Lay down." She grabbed one of the decorative couch pillows covered in silhouettes of deer, put it near her, and patted it. "You heard me—grab your covers and come put your head here and I'll teach you the secret to falling asleep."

That sounded very unlikely but he did it, spreading out lengthwise on the couch instead of on the chaise so his head was close to hers. As soon as he did, she got back into her previous position, snuggled upon her side facing him so that together they formed an *L*.

"Close your eyes and picture a porch swing," she said, her voice more of a whisper than its usual volume.

"This isn't going to work." None of it ever did.

She flicked him in the shoulder with her fingers. "Not if you're talking."

"Fine." He closed his eyes and his mouth.

"With each inhale, the swing goes back and with each exhale it goes forward," she said, each word calm and deliberate, without sounding like a carnival hypnotist. "Keep your breaths slow and steady so it just gently swings in the breeze. Back and forth and back and forth."

He'd tried meditation and visualizations before. None had worked, but there was something about Shelby and the higher pitch of her voice that settled him. It didn't make any sense. It was supposed to be lower voices that soothed, but he couldn't deny that his eyes were getting heavy the longer they lay there, their breaths syncing as he imagined a white porch swing moving back and forth.

"I like listening to you talk," he said, the words coming out before he could second-guess.

"No one likes that," she said, her voice soft and sleepy. "There's a reason why I do most of my talking from a keyboard, because otherwise I'm The Squeaker."

Her voice wasn't *that* high-pitched. Jesus. "People are assholes."

A barely there scoff in agreement. "They can be."

In and out, he concentrated on the sound of his breathing, making sure to match her inhales and exhales, as the fire crackled in the distance. It was better than any option on his white-noise app.

"Shelby?"

She mumbled something that might have been an acknowledgment that she was still sort of awake, or it could have been a half snore—he had no fucking clue.

"Thank you."

If she was still awake to hear it, he couldn't tell, and he was about half a second from joining her anyway.

...

It was still way-too-damn-early-o'clock, according to her body, when Shelby woke up trying to figure out who she was, let alone where she was. It came back to her in bits and pieces as she blinked the room into focus. Ian was hunkered down in front of the fireplace, a cast-iron pan in his oven-mitt grip and the unmistakable scent of bacon in the air. Suddenly, some parts of her were more awake than others.

Sure, she could pretend it was because of the bacon—who didn't love bacon?—but that wasn't it. Thank God he was turned away from her, because if he could see her face right now, she had no doubts he'd know every single one of the dirty thoughts she was having about him.

Maybe you should have stuck with Mediocre Matt for longer so you wouldn't be perving off seeing a guy cooking over an open fire.

Nah, the whole line about how sex was like pizza, even when it was bad it was good, pretty much applied only to the bro-dudes-in-finance kind of person. Six months of occasional orgasms while banging Mediocre Matt on the regular had taught her that. There was no way she was going to rethink her decision to send him packing.

Ian put the skillet down on a grate in the fireplace and turned around. Her brain hollered at her to play it cool, but her whole body did a hello-good-morning-to-me shiver of appreciation.

"Are you cold?" he asked as he stretched his arms and rolled his neck from side to side.

No, she most definitely was not; watching the way his muscles moved as he lifted his arms and brought them across his chest was mesmerizing. "I'm good. You like to cook?"

"I like to eat, so cooking is part of it." He turned back to the skillet, flipping the bacon and then cracking two eggs into the pan.

"What can I do?" she asked, throwing back the covers and getting up before she realized her sleep pants had worked their way down—waaaaaaaay down—in the middle of the night.

Ian glanced back over his shoulder at her and froze. His gaze dropped to her exposed lower belly and lingered for two breaths too long as he worked his jaw back and forth before his focus traveled slowly up her body.

Her breath caught as she stood there, feeling naked under his attention, as electricity zinged through her and touched every nerve ending. Her nipples pebbled under her thermal underwear that left pretty much nothing to the imagination when it came to her high beams. She had to clasp her hands together to resist the urge to touch them, to roll their peaks between her fingers to dull the building ache inside her.

Ian turned back around, his shoulders stiff, then said, "You can get the plates."

Hitching up her pants while trying to make it look like she wasn't, she crossed the living room. "From the kitchen? Yeah, sure, sure, the kitchen. I will get them."

Way to sound like you aren't a giant weirdo, Shelby girl.

Like there was any hope of that around Ian Petrov.

Beyond his scruffy hotness, he was from hockey royalty. She knew his stats, his pregame meal preferences, and she'd let slip his deepest secret—one he hadn't even known he had. So yeah, she would never be able to just act normal around him. And with that reminder, the idea of breakfast became totally unappealing.

After delivering a plate, bottle of water, napkin, and utensils, she gathered up some clothes in a bundle and headed toward the bathroom. "You go ahead without me."

He looked down at the single place setting on the coffee table. "You're not eating?"

"The snow stopped, so I'm gonna go see if I can shovel my car out and get out of your hair." And yeah, she needed to get out of here before she made an idiot of herself by getting caught ogling him.

"The roads aren't safe," he said as he took the cast-iron skillet off the grate and slid the eggs and bacon onto the waiting plate.

"Well, once they are, I'll be all ready." Yeah, that sounded totally believable and not at all like she needed a snowbank between them to get her wayward body back under control.

He let out a rumbling sigh. "Is it because being here alone with me makes you uncomfortable?"

Not in the way he was thinking. She caught herself staring at the vee lines that disappeared under his waistband and jerked her focus back up to his face where it should have been the whole time.

"It's not that." She started toward the bathroom again. "Lucy obviously made a mistake, and I'm the one who should leave when the roads are better. You had plans that didn't involve me, and I'll let you get back to them."

"And I can't change your mind?"

She plastered on a cheery smile that she hoped didn't look totally off-kilter. "Nope."

Nodding, he shrugged. "Okay, then."

She hadn't expected him to give in so easily, but she'd take the victory. Making good on her win, she hurried off to the bathroom to change. By the time she got back, Ian was nowhere to be seen. A frigid blast of air hit her as soon as she stepped out onto the porch and reached for where the shovel had been the night before. It was gone. That's when she spotted Ian still in those shouldn't-be-sexy-but-were blue pants and a thick parka shoveling out his car.

Victory? More like total subterfuge!

Oh no. That is not how this is supposed to go. I'm the one who should be shoveling out my car.

She marched over, sticking to the narrow path he'd cleared between the porch and the vehicles, and held out her hand. "My shovel, please."

He lifted it above his head where she had no hopes of reaching it unless she climbed him like a tree, which—as tempting as it was—she was not going to do because she had some pride left.

"The roads aren't safe yet," he said, as if that explained his overprotective-bordering-on-patronizing actions.

"What, you think I'm going to squeal off, leaving nothing but burned rubber on the snowpack?" She planted her hands on her hips and glared up at him. "I don't have a death wish."

"Good, then I'll clear out my car, and I'll leave when the roads clear up so you don't have to drive on the roads."

She held out her hand again, just like last night when she'd checked his thumb. "Give me the shovel."

"If you want it, you'll have to take it," Ian said.

Of all the high-handed things. It wasn't fair. She was taking the high road. She was giving him the cabin. She was going to win.

"This isn't fair," she said.

He just shrugged.

Frustration winning out, Shelby grabbed a handful of snow and shoved it right in Ian's face. She had three seconds of oh-shit-what-did-I-just-do making her pulse spike before he started laughing. He didn't drop the shovel, though; he put it on the roof of his car and grinned down at her.

"Oh, you want to have a snowball fight? It's on," he said as he cleared the snow from his face. "You've got a five-second head start."

Giddy adrenaline pumping through her veins, she took off looking for cover, bending over and scooping up a handful of snow as she went. She almost made it to the porch when a snowball landed with a *thwat* in the middle of her back. Turning, she let fly the half-formed one in her hand. Ian dodged it easily, but that attack gave her time to get up to the porch, which may have less snow than the yard but had better coverage.

"You realize you're trapped," he hollered from behind his car.

"I have the high ground and access to the house," she shot back. "I could lock you out."

He shot off three quick snowballs. "You wouldn't."

"Not for a long time, anyway." Really, not at all, but it wasn't like he didn't know that already.

He laughed and shot off another snowball, but it went wide, hitting the front door with a splat. And so it went, snowballs flying through the air as he circled the porch, dodging her limited-supply snowballs. The rest of it all didn't matter. For the moment, there wasn't a world beyond their little snowed-in patch of earth, and Shelby gave in to the absolute joy of that freedom.

That anxious feeling always in the bottom of her gut, the one that had kept her from walking into the media room a few weeks ago, it shrank into nearly nothing. There was only here and now. Before, that had only happened in the moment between buzzed and drunk that she'd tried to ride for way too long. This was so much better. In the mix of everything, she'd forgotten how to let go and just have fun.

By the time they were out of snowballs, Shelby had snow

down her shirt, her socks were soaked to her toes, her fingers were half frozen, and her cheeks hurt from laughing so hard. After kicking off the snow stuck to their boots outside, they shucked them off just inside the door, leaving them on the thick weatherproof mat, and hurried to the fireplace to start to defrost.

"I've got to get out of this," she said. "Turn around. No peeking."

Ian grunted in agreement, his shirt already half off. Fighting the urge to freeze to death so she could watch him finish taking off his shirt, she turned and faced the staircase. Getting off wet jeans with icicle hands was second only to trying to take off a sweaty sports bra on her worst-clothes-to-remove list, but she managed. By the time she had on a pair of yoga pants, a long-sleeve T-shirt, and a pair of wooly socks, she'd started getting feeling back in her toes.

"Is it safe to turn around?" she asked.

"You're clear," he said.

She turned and nearly ran into Ian, he was so close. He was mismatched in joggers and a fisherman's sweater, the thick cream-colored kind that made her fingers itch to touch him—it! She wanted to touch the sweater, not him. Really. Sorta. Maybe. Oh God, not at all.

He took her hands in his, cupping them and bringing them up to his mouth to blow on them. "You're freezing."

"My gloves weren't made for snowball fights." The knit gloves had been soaked through by her third snowball. "I hadn't been planning on going to war."

"I'd better warm you up, then." He brought her hands to his mouth again, blowing on her knuckles.

It wasn't even a touch, but it sent a wave of scorching-hot desire slamming into her that made her forget all of the very good reasons why this was a very bad idea. "What are your plans for getting me warm?"

Her hard nipples pressing against the thin material of her tank top were directly at eye level. She could blame it on the cold, but her body was hot, overheated, even—and it had nothing to do with the temperature.

A mewling sigh sounded in her ears, soft and needy. It took her a second to realize the sound had come from her. Her hands still in his, he glanced up at her, his eyes dark with a possessive lust that made her core clench.

She wanted to straddle him, ride him, feel his cock rub up against every sensitive spot at the apex of her legs. She wanted to take him inside her, press her palms against the hard ridges of his abs, and ride him slow and sure. She wanted to be under him on the bed, pressed up against him with the wall at her back, and on her hands and knees as he pounded into her like she craved each time her fingers slid between her slick folds.

"Shelby..." He made her name sound like a naughty promise and a desperate plea as he stripped off his sweater. He let her hands go, obviously giving her the space to make the call. "How hot do you want to get?"

Tempting. So damn tempting. Her fingertips were tracing the line of his jaw, the coarse hair scraping her tender flesh before she even realized what she was doing. He didn't touch her in return. He waited—patient, enticing, confident—letting her take the lead, as if he already knew what she'd say next. It wasn't triumph in his dark eyes but pure focused need—all of it directed at her. It was incendiary to be at the center of it, and she was going up in flames.

She traced the line of his throat and across his corded shoulders, the whole time feeling like a woman who'd made this decision a million years ago and was only now admitting it. "No one could know, and it would have to be a different-zip-code-only thing."

"There's no one here I'd ever tell," he said, his voice

strained with need.

The springy hairs dusting his pecs tickled her fingers as she continued her explorations. "It can't be anything more than just sex, and only this one time. You hockey players are off-limits for corporate."

Okay, that was more for herself than Ian. It wasn't like someone like him had ever had problems separating orgasms from something more.

"We might be snowed in for days," he said, his eyes fluttering shut for a second as she traced her way downward, following his narrow happy trail. "And nobody's on the clock here."

She hesitated at the waistband of his joggers, her nipples so hard, they hurt. "Ian…"

"God, I love the way you say my name."

Just the rumble of his words was enough to make her clit quiver with anticipation, but he still didn't make a single move to touch her. She knew why. He wanted her to make the first move, to have control, to show him just how much she wanted him. The moment was as empowering as it was sexually frustrating.

"Ian, please." She hooked her fingers in the waistband of his joggers. "I wanna get really hot."

Cupping the back of her head, he dipped his head lower, his mouth centimeters from hers, hovering there above her so close, she could feel him even without actually touching him. Another opportunity to back out? To run? It didn't matter, because she wasn't going anywhere right now. It only took the slightest move to press her lips to his in a kiss, and she let herself fall back into the delicious pleasure of it all.

Chapter Six

Kissing Shelby hadn't been part of Ian's plan after their impromptu snowball fight. He was supposed to get dressed, give her space, and wait for the roads to clear so he could be the one to drive away from the cabin hideaway. He'd gotten a look at the tires on her car when he'd walked outside with the shovel. They were as bald as his first juniors coach, who'd gotten cans of car wax every Christmas as a gag gift from the team.

Dammit, Ian had been trying to be a gentleman, to make up for being such an asshole to her before. And yeah, he'd been on a mission to save himself from doing just this because there was no way it was a good idea. But she tasted so sweet, and when she made that soft moan and parted her lips, he was fucking gone. Hands skimming the slightly round curve of her ass, he cupped it and pulled her tight against him, taking her down to the rug in front of the fireplace, settling her so she straddled his lap. The teasing heat of her through the thin, stretchy material of her yoga pants pressing against his hard cock under his joggers wasn't nearly enough.

He needed more. He needed all of her.

She broke the kiss, her lips swollen and her eyes hazy as she tugged up her shirt, yanking it off and letting it fall to the floor. He let out a harsh hiss of breath. She was bare underneath, the tips of her firm tits hardened to pink points.

Skimming her fingertips across his chest so lightly it almost felt like a dream, she wet her lips with the tip of her pink tongue. His cock twitched in anticipation of what she was going to do next. Hell, just watching that mouth of hers might kill him.

Then she undulated her hips, rolling them so her core rubbed against his length and electricity shot straight to his dick. He grabbed her by the hips, holding her to him as she rocked, the friction almost enough but not even close at the same time. Her fingers bit into his shoulders as she leaned down, kissing him, demanding everything, and he was more than willing to give it. Taking his opportunity, he grabbed her hips and flipped her so she was under him.

All he could feel was the softness of Shelby's lips on his, the sweet curve of her waist where it flared out to meet his and—even with the barrier of his joggers and her yoga pants between them—the slick heat of her pressed against his dick. How their clothing didn't go up in flames the moment he sank between her thighs and ground against her, he had no clue. Especially not when she moaned into his mouth, her teeth grazing his bottom lip. Oh, somebody liked that. He did it again, this time changing the angle just enough that if he was lucky, he'd stroke the head of his cock against her clit. She arched against him, letting her head fall back into the pillow, and let out a lusty groan that made his balls tingle. Oh yeah, that was the kind of sound he loved hearing from her.

"I could probably come just from hearing you moan like that," he said, kissing his way down the column of her throat to the sensitive spot at the base.

She rotated her hips, rubbing herself against him. "I need a little more than that."

"Don't worry. You'll be getting it."

He cupped her breast and dragged his thumb across the stiff peak. Shelby groaned, and he repeated the move again and again until her skin was flush with desire. Then he leaned down and sucked her nipple into his mouth, drawing on it. Her hands were in his hair, digging into his scalp at the back of his head and holding him in place as he teased and tugged on her sensitive flesh.

"Ian, please," she pleaded.

"Do you want more or less?" he asked, praying that it wasn't less, because he already knew he wouldn't be able to get enough of her tonight.

"All of it," she said, her heady voice strained with desire. "Right now."

"Not yet. I want to get my fill of you, tasting every inch of your skin, sinking my tongue between your thighs, and making your come all over my lips before I even sink my dick inside your tight pussy." All of that. That's what he wanted.

There was something delicious seeing Shelby undone like this, moaning beneath him on the rug and rubbing herself against him as he rolled and pulled her nipples with just the right amount of tension to elicit little moans of pleasure from her. Her fingernails dug into his ass and she hooked her legs around the back of his thighs, holding him hard against her—as if there was any other place he wanted to be.

Swirling his tongue around her extended nipple, he pressed against her damp center. Fuck. This was going to kill him. He'd come in his joggers if he didn't give his aching cock a time-out. While coming with Shelby would be good, coming inside her and feeling her tighten around him would be so much better. So he untangled himself from her legs and slid lower down her body, sliding her yoga pants over her hips as he went lower. Then he sat back on his heels and looked at the woman spread out before him.

"God, you're beautiful. I could look at you all night."

She glided her hand over her body, over her tits, down her flat stomach, and through the tight ebony curls between her thighs. The house could explode around them and he wouldn't have been able to look away from her at this moment—something her knowing chuckle acknowledged. It took some effort, but he tore his gaze away from her pussy and back to her face.

"Yes, I'm definitely getting warmer, but I'm pretty sure I can get even hotter."

"Is that a challenge from that snarky mouth of yours?" And his was dry at the moment. There was only so much a man could take, watching this little performance of hers.

She reached out to him, her fingers finding the elastic waistband of his pants. "You could always give me something else to taste."

"Soon, but you're too pretty not to taste," he said, barely recognizing his own voice in the words of a man skating the edge of desperation.

Following his fingers, he dipped his head between her legs and traced his tongue down her center, relishing her responsive moan. It wasn't enough, though. He wanted to feel her come. He spread her wide open with his fingers and devoted every bit of his fractured concentration to making her break apart. Licking, sucking, teasing, sliding one and then two fingers deep inside her, he drove her higher and higher until her thighs were quaking.

"Ian," she moaned. "Don't stop."

He wasn't planning on it, not when he had her so close that all she could do was lose herself in the feeling of it all. The angle of their position didn't allow him the luxury of watching her face as she moved higher and higher; instead, he had to judge her reaction by the pitch of her moans and the shiver of her thighs. When her core muscles gripped his fingers in a rhythmic pulse that built with every stroke in and out, her core squeezed his fingers tight as she came, her entire body arching against him. Her moan of pleasure reverberated against his cock, making his balls tug up close to his body. It was exquisite torture, beating any imaginings he'd had.

"Oh my God," she said, rolling onto her back, her breathing erratic. "That was just what I needed."

• • •

Shelby was going to die a happy woman from all of this pleasure. But if she lived? Damn she'd be one lucky woman.

"Glad I could be of service," he said between long, leisurely kisses.

"Oh, you're not done." Her fingertips skated down his body.

"I'm not?"

Her hand wrapped around his hard length. "I have condoms."

"Hope you have enough of them." Ian rolled her hard nipple to a stiff peak. "I can't wait to feel you come all over my cock again and again."

Keeping her mouth busy exploring the line of his jaw as they lay side by side facing each other, Shelby deliberately stroked her hand up and down his hot length. It turned his words into a desperate groan that had her doing it again—only even slower. What could she say, there was just something about being in control of giving that kind of pleasure that turned her on. Leaning forward, she trailed kisses across his broad chest, dipping down from the top of his pecs to his flat nipples. The temptation to continue her way south made her mouth dry, but that's not what she wanted. Not right now.

"Get on your back."

A wry chuckle rumbled from his chest beneath her lips, but he complied. "You're demanding."

"And you better stay like that until I get back." She got up and made a quick trip to the bathroom for a condom from her toiletry bag. When she got back, he was still lounging lazily stroking his cock. "You're very good at following directions."

"And what if I want to lead?" he asked, his hooded gaze traveling across her naked body as solid as a touch.

"You have to wait your turn." Giving him a saucy look, she ripped the foil packet and took out the latex condom.

"Are you always this much of a hard-ass?" The question came out sure and cocky right up until the last two words, which just happened to be when she rolled the condom over his prick with deliberate care.

She didn't bother to hide her grin. "When I know what I want, yes."

A vein in his jaw twitched, but he didn't make a move. "And what is it that you want?"

"This." Tilting her hips a few degrees, she slid all the way down his length, letting her head fall back as she relished the feeling of oh-my-God-yes-that-is-amazing making her bite down on her bottom lip. It had officially been too long, because there was no way Ian should feel that good inside her, as if this was how sex was always supposed to feel.

His hands were on her hips a heartbeat later, tugging her forward, making her clit rub against him on each downward stroke. "Touch your tits."

"Now who's being demanding?" she asked, but her hands were cupping her breasts before the words were even out of his mouth.

The second she started rolling her nipples between her fingers, he inhaled a sharp breath and his fingers bit into her hips. Oh, he liked that, did he? Never taking her eyes off his face as she rocked herself up and down his thick cock, the move making her thighs ache at the same time it sent shivers of pleasure through her body, she pinched her nipples and tugged hard on them.

His brown eyes darkened with lust so primal, it sent a thrill right to her clit. "I'm claiming my turn."

Without losing their connection, he shifted underneath her, tilting her until her back was on the rug and he was on his knees, with her feet planted on the floor on either side of his thighs. Oh hell yes. She arched her body, bringing her hips higher and in line with his. His hands cupped her ass, each finger digging into her flesh with just the right amount of pleasure as he pistoned his hips, plunging into her, filling her so completely that it stole her breath.

"So damn tight, so wet, so hot," he said, pushing into her with each declaration. "You feel so fucking good."

If she could speak at that moment, she would have returned the compliment, but as it was, she wasn't sure she could speak right then. She was already too far gone.

His hands moved from her ass to her back and he lifted her upper body until her breasts were pressed against his chest, never once losing his rhythm. She wrapped her arms around his corded neck and met every one of his thrusts with a swirl of her hips as she climbed toward her orgasm. Her grip tightened and she leaned back, changing the angle so his cock stroked the sensitive bundle of nerves just inside her opening with every stroke.

He let out a possessive growl. "Look at how wet you've made my dick."

She glanced down. Fuck. She could see herself on him and it was one of the hottest things she'd ever seen.

"Ian." She wanted to say more, but that one syllable was all that she could get out. The sensations building in her core were like a ball of megawatt electricity growing with each thrust and retreat, making it almost impossible to do anything but chase after her climax.

"Say it again." He plunged into her harder, deeper.

"Ian." Breathy. Begging. On the verge.

"Jesus, Shelby, I'm gonna come." He slipped his hand between their bodies and rolled her clit with the pad of his thumb, round and round.

The pleasure built and built until— "Oh. My. God."

And she broke apart as her orgasm crashed into her, turning her entire body electric. Ian sank back onto his heels, taking her with him and shoving her up and down his length in an ever faster rhythm before sinking deep within her and coming with a harsh groan.

She was floating and sinking at the same time as she collapsed against him, secure at least in this moment, that he'd catch her. And he did, wrapping his arms around her and holding her tight as they both came down.

Four hundred and sixty-eight days later—or at least that's what it felt like—her heart rate finally returned to normal and she slid off him and back onto the rug. She swore her eyes didn't flicker shut, but the next thing she was aware of was Ian scooping her up from the floor and carrying her to the couch. He'd made up one of the chaise ends with blankets and two pillows. He laid her down and then scooted in beside her.

"Where'd you go?" she asked, trying to regain her mental footing.

"Got rid of the condom." He grabbed the grizzly-bear comforter and threw it over both of them, then pulled her in close so her head was resting on his chest. "Now, rest up. I was serious about taking advantage of being snowed in. I have plans for us tomorrow."

Even as sleep tugged at her, she knew that she should remind him this was a one-time-only thing. Hell, she should probably be reminding herself. She would. Tomorrow. Tonight, she was going to enjoy the post-orgasm snuggle.

Chapter Seven

"You're gonna wanna get up real slowly and make sure I can see your hands."

If there was anything that would make Shelby wake up in an instant, it was those words spoken by an unfamiliar voice. Heart hammering, she sat straight up, clutching the comforter to her chest. Ian shifted so his body blocked hers from the older couple in head-to-toe plaid flannel—including matching fuzzy hats with ear flaps—and the sheriff's deputy. The trio stood in front of the fireplace right next to a large framed photo on the mantel showing the same older couple surrounded by about a million grandkids ranging from toddlers to college-age.

"There's obviously been some kind of mistake," Ian said, clearly making an effort to keep the situation calm. "Officer, we haven't done anything wrong."

"Nothing wrong? Nothing wrong! You just thought you could get away with it again, huh?" the man said. "Well, this time we caught you, and we have the video surveillance. I hope you like jail, because we are most definitely pressing charges."

Jail? Charges? Video? A frigid blast of fear went straight through her, and she pulled the blanket tighter around her bare shoulders. "What's going on, Ian?"

"No fucking clue," he grumbled. "Stay behind me."

The man let out a sharp, crowing laugh. "You finally got caught—that's what's going on."

The deputy who barely looked like he could grow a full mustache kept his hand loosely on his holstered service weapon and turned his attention to Ian and Shelby. "Mr. and Mrs. Morgan received a silent-alarm call prior to the storm. Once the storm had passed, they contacted the sheriff's department and requested assistance."

"Listen to you," Mrs. Morgan said, turning to the deputy with a proud smile. "You sound just like a real law-enforcement officer."

"Mom," the deputy said with a sigh. "I've been on the force for eight months now."

"And we couldn't be prouder of our baby boy." She clapped, making the charms on her bracelet rattle. "Look at you making your first arrest. Your father wanted to call the sheriff himself, but I told him no, this could make Alan's career. You've arrested the cabin bandits!"

"Arrest?" Shelby nearly jumped up but then remembered that one, she had no clothes on and two, that might not be the best idea when facing a fresh-behind-the-ears deputy with his hand on his gun. "Who's getting arrested? And who are you? What is going on?"

"Like you don't know," Mr. Morgan said, chest puffing out. "Sure, the first time we thought maybe we were mistaken, the second time the upstairs beds had definitely been slept in, and the third time half the groceries were gone and liquor cabinet emptied. That's when I added the bear."

He pointed to a stuffed bear set on the bookshelves under

the staircase. It looked like a normal bear, but judging by the absolute glee in Mr. Morgan's eyes, it was not. Nanny cam. Had to be. And it was pointed so it would catch everything from the front door to the fireplace to the couch.

Her stomach dropped way past her toes down to the core of the earth.

Oh. My. God.

She had a sex tape. Embarrassment burned her cheeks. Beside her, Ian stiffened, every muscle in his back tensing and his jaw going so square as he clamped his teeth together that someone could probably use it to measure a ninety-degree angle.

"You're very flexible," Mrs. Morgan said, looking past Ian and right at Shelby. "Enjoy it while you're young. Pretty soon you try some of that and your hip is just going to go straight out."

The deputy turned almost as red as Shelby. "Mom."

"Sorry, Alan, but it's true," Mrs. Morgan said with a shrug before turning her attention back to Shelby. "And don't worry. Clyde didn't watch, and I made sure to edit what we got off the cloud so it ended when things got—ahem—heated."

Her focus slid over to Ian, and she let out a little sigh.

"Okay, we need to bring this back to the matter at hand," Alan said, pulling out a notebook, his hands shaking just the slightest bit. "I'm gonna need identification from both of you."

"Wallet's on the table," Ian said in his all-too-familiar gruff rumble. "We each have a rental agreement for the cabin. We are not trespassing and I sure as hell do not appreciate being under surveillance."

"Like we would rent out our family cabin," Mr. Morgan harrumphed. "Not in this lifetime."

Eyes wide, Shelby exchanged a worried look with Ian. Not a rental? That wasn't right. It couldn't be. What kind of weird-ass game were these people playing at? They had good cop, bad cop, and actual cop, but none of it made sense.

"Your identification, miss?" Alan asked.

"My driver's license is in my phone case," Shelby said, a shot of nervous panic making her shiver.

"Can we at least get some clothes while we do this?" Ian asked.

"Oh my Lord, you must be freezing," Mrs. Morgan said as she reached down and picked up a pile of their clothes on the floor in front of the fireplace and started walking toward them.

"Faith," Mr. Morgan grumbled. "They could attack you."

Mrs. Morgan eyeballed Ian. "Imagine that."

While they got dressed under the covers and the watchful gazes of the Morgans, Alan opened up Ian's wallet and pulled out his driver's license.

"Petrov?" Mr. Morgan asked after peeking over his son's shoulder. "What is that, Russian? You some kind of spy?"

"Hockey player," Ian said.

Mr. Morgan scoffed. "We watch good American football up here."

"Baseball in the summer," Mrs. Morgan added.

"That's right, and baseball in the summer."

The deputy glared his parents into silence. "You have a copy of your rental agreement?"

"They're on our phones and they're out of juice," Shelby said.

Alan rubbed his chin as he glanced around the cabin. "Okay, well, let's head down to the station to get all of this worked out."

"Don't you have to read them their rights, honey?" Mrs. Morgan patted her son's forearm. "They always do that on TV when they're arresting someone."

"I'm not arresting them, Mom."

"Why not?" Mr. Morgan demanded.

"Because I'm taking everyone back down to the station so they can charge their phones and we can figure out what is going on before making any arrests."

"Oh, that's very smart." Mrs. Morgan looked over at Shelby. "He gets the brains from my side. Albert here is guided by his passions. It can be overwhelming at times but also very worth it. I'm sure you know what I mean."

Shelby squeaked—literally—out something that sort of sounded like an answer, and a few minutes later, they'd gathered all their stuff and were piling into a truck with a sheriff's logo painted on the side and a snowplow attachment on the front. Ian and Shelby took the back while all the Morgans took the front seats, and they headed down the mountain. Heart racing as she drummed her fingers on the space between them, Shelby looked over at Ian, trying for a we're-gonna-be-okay smile and failing miserably. Mug shots were very much not her thing. Ian let out a soft signature grunt and took her hand—and some of the tension in her shoulders eased a bit. She wasn't alone in this. And the fact that that made her feel so good let her know that she was in trouble, because whatever had happened between them had to stay at that cabin.

...

The Buffly County Sheriff's Office break room had fresh coffee, actual heat coming out of the vents, and—best of all—electricity. Sure, Ian's screen was a mass of spidery cracks, but all he needed was for there to be enough visible screen to read the email Lucy had sent that would clear up this mess. He plugged in his phone using the cord Deputy Alan handed him.

"Don't suppose you have an iPhone Four charger?"

Shelby asked, the contents of her oversize purse scattered about on one end of the break room table. "I swear I packed mine, but it's not in my bag."

"You have a Four?" Ian and Alan shared a what-the-fuck eyebrow raise.

"Hey, don't mock." She started tossing things back into her bag. Notepad. Six pens. Three ChapSticks. Hand sanitizer. So many gum wrappers. "It works great. I also have a regular Crock-Pot, a top-loading washer, and the first-generation Kindle Paperwhite. I like what I like."

"Sorry," Alan said with a cough that sounded a lot like he was trying to cover up a laugh. "I only have the lightning chargers. I'll ask around. Someone might have one in a drawer somewhere, but we're running on a skeleton crew with the storm and all."

Mrs. Morgan—still giving him the hey-baby eye—sat down across from him with a cup of coffee, steam rising up from the mug. Her husband took the seat next to her, ignoring the mug in his hands in favor of glaring at Ian and Shelby.

"Well, mine should have enough power soon to show the email," he said, turning his attention to Alan and not his way-too-intense-for-different-reasons parents. "Lucy sent us the same one for Six Melchers Way."

"Six?" Mr. Morgan asked.

Shelby nodded. "Yeah."

"Our family cabin is number nine," Mrs. Morgan said before taking a sip of her coffee.

"No, I definitely saw the sign at the end of the drive even in the snow." It had been dark and the wind had picked up, but there had been no missing the weathered sign with the big wooden number hanging from it. "It said six."

"Albert," Mrs. Morgan said, her lips flattening into a tight line. "You didn't really fix it, did you? I have asked and asked and you told me you'd taken care of it."

A teenage girl in a Buffly Sheriff's Office volunteer shirt came in then, delivering a plate of doughnuts. Ian snagged one with sprinkles while Shelby got the double chocolate. None of the Morgans took one. They were all too caught up in what sounded like an argument that had been raging for years.

"I hooked it up to the old nail. Bree was with me when I did it," the older man said, nodding at the volunteer. "Sure, it was wobbly, but it worked."

"Yeah, right up until a storm started to blow in," Shelby said, earning a thank-you-very-much nod of agreement from Mrs. Morgan. "So if you're number nine, then where is number six?"

"That was the old Wilkes place," Alan said, finally reaching for a doughnut. "I think their kids did put it on the the rental listings. They don't have a sign, though, and if you came through when it was snowing, their drive is easy to miss. Even locals miss it sometimes."

Ian glanced over at Shelby, expecting to see her at least shaking her head in amazement at everything that had happened to get them both at the same cabin before the storm. But instead of relaxed and amused, she was drawn up tight, her fingers doing that nervous drumming thing on her thigh as she chewed her bottom lip. He reached for her hand again, like he had in the truck, but this time she slipped free of his grasp.

He was trying to process the change when Mr. Morgan tapped the table in front of Ian.

"That cleared that up," the older man said. "But if you two weren't crashing our cabin during the weekends, then who was?"

"Someone was at your place, Gramps?" The girl in the volunteer shirt nearly stuffed a whole doughnut in her mouth but kept talking around it. "That's just wild. What makes you think someone was there? I mean, it's not like you two go up in the winter."

All the Morgans sitting at the table turned and put the teen in their view.

"Bree," Alan said. "What do you know?"

The girl shrank down in her chair, swallowed the doughnut, and pulled up the round collar of her T-shirt over her mouth. "Nothing."

"Bree Elizabeth Morgan," Mrs. Morgan said in the type of voice that no one with any sense would argue with. "You better spill it, young lady."

"We only went up there a couple of times. I used the hidden key Grandpa showed me when we fixed the sign and then just left it unlocked." It came out as a wail, a pitiful teenage I've-been-caught wail. "It was only a small group of us, but then a bunch of people heard and half of my class was there. It was like one of those movies, but I swear no one threw up on the couch and the bunny statue got knocked over by accident before they found the key to the liquor cabinet."

"Young lady, we are going to go have a chat with your parents. Let's go." Mrs. Morgan's chair squeaked on the linoleum floor when she pushed it back and stood, pointing her granddaughter to the door. "I'm so sorry about the confusion—and the video."

"You've got to delete it and hand over this copy," Ian said.

She nodded in agreement and then had the grace to look shame-faced as she and her husband led their wayward granddaughter out of the room, each of them talking over the other with the girl's plaintive whining ribboning through it. Yeah, Ian had been there. Neither of his parents had put up with shit, but he'd tried his best anyway. It was his mom who usually caught him and set him straight, especially since his dad spent most of Ian's childhood on the road.

Yeah, having a second family and banging whichever

other puck bunnies he came across.

His good mood disappeared and before he'd exhaled, he was feeling just as salty as Shelby was looking sitting next to him. And what was that all about? They'd gone to bed happy, and then everything had gone to shit. It didn't make a damn bit of sense, but then again, when did anything involving his life ever?

"My sister is going to ground that girl until she's eighty," Alan said, shaking his head. "Sorry for the trouble. Give me a couple of minutes and I'll get you two back up the mountain. I'm happy to bring you over to the Wilkes place."

"Actually," Shelby said, her voice going up even higher than usual as she looked down at her hands clasped together in her lap. "I think it might be best if I head back to Harbor City."

Ian flinched. "Why?"

She didn't look over at him, instead keeping her attention on her hands. "I can prep for work and maybe go in Monday and get a head start before the new job officially starts on Tuesday."

He stopped himself, just barely, from pointing out that it was only Saturday because he already felt like he'd been cross-checked into the boards. There was no reason to beg for her attention. They'd both gotten what they wanted, had fun, and now it was over. Just like they'd agreed. Great. Perfect. Fucking amazing. He couldn't be happier.

Yeah, that's totally believable if you don't have two brain cells to rub together.

"I think this is for the best," she said, her words coming out in a rush. "I'll shovel my rental out and head back to the city. You stay. Enjoy the cabin just like you'd planned."

Suddenly, a few days alone to drown himself in a bottle of scotch and feel sorry for himself seemed like the most miserable self-indulgent activity ever. It was fucking whiny.

He might as well be a soccer player going into dramatics because he'd gotten bumped into on the field.

"I'll head back, too," he said. "I've lost interest in a weekend in the mountains."

"You have a rental?" Alan asked, snagging a doughnut for himself.

"Yeah," she said. "I don't need a car in the city."

"Is it a four-wheel drive?"

She shook her head. "I never thought there'd be a snowstorm this late in the year."

He made a *tsk-tsk* sound. "Then I recommend you call someone to come get you down here. It might be a week before we can get the mountain roads plowed well enough for regular cars to travel safely." He got up from the table and walked over to the coffee maker, pouring himself a cup. "Is there someone you can call to come pick you up? The local rental folks can get the rental once the snow melts. They do it all the time. Trust me, you are not the first tourists to find yourselves on the bad side of Mother Nature around here."

Shelby looked down at her phone that was, for all intents and purposes, a very expensive door stopper at the moment. "I don't know anyone's number anymore."

Ian reached for his phone and powered it on. "I can bring up someone with the team's front office who can help. It would serve Lucy right if she had to come up here and get us."

After fifteen eternity-lasting seconds, it came on. However, staring down at the Ice Knights logo on his home screen was like viewing it through a kaleidoscope. And when he hit the touchscreen, nothing happened.

"Don't suppose the car rental place is open now?" Ian asked.

Alan shook his head. "Buck's on vacation in Florida, the lucky son of a bitch. It's closed until next week."

Ian bit back a groan. There were two numbers Ian knew

by heart. His parents' landline and his former best friend's cell. He hadn't dialed either of them for weeks, didn't want to call either of them for the foreseeable future, if ever. But he and Shelby were stuck. He didn't have a choice. He had to pick the lesser of two assholes. Hating it, he picked up the phone and dialed Christensen.

Chapter Eight

Shelby was standing in the sheriff's office lobby in front of the glass doors already bundled up in her coat and more than ready to get the hell out of there when a black SUV with Ice Knights vanity plates pulled into the partially plowed parking lot. Relief seeped into her shoulders and she relaxed them about halfway down from touching her earlobes. Why only halfway? Because OMG, the tension flowing off Ian even though he was on the other side of the lobby was strong enough to be a battering ram.

So much for their tentative truce. He'd gone totally grumpsterville on her again. Was he regretting last night? God knew the smart part of her was, even if she knew it could never work out between them. He was a hockey star; she worked for the team. How in the hell was she supposed to cover the team if she was fucking one of the players? Not to mention, he was all about the snarl and believing everything was at its worst. She had to believe that there was always a silver lining; if she didn't have that inside her, she wasn't sure she would have made it through rehab. It was the right call to limit sex to the cabin. They'd gotten it out of their system.

Still...it sure would have been nice to have another few nights on that rug.

Of course, that didn't mean he couldn't just take the surly down a couple of notches. They weren't enemies, just former onetime lovers.

Thanks to the power of reflections, she was able to watch the SUV park in one of the empty spots and see the lines in Ian's forehead deepen as he squared his jaw. She took half a step back toward him before she caught herself.

Clean breaks were the best kind. If she didn't, she'd get tangled up in feelings that were one-sided, and that way lay trouble. There were things she could control and things she couldn't. The best option for her was to stick with what she could control.

Forcing her gaze away from Ian, because the man was the word "uncontrollable" in human form, she closed her eyes and took a deep breath to center herself. Okay, this drive home was not going to be fun, but at least she'd have the back seat to herself while Ian and Alex did their awkward no-talking thing. Or they would fight the whole drive back. Even worse, it could be hours of passive-aggressive snipping back and forth at each other until they got back to Harbor City.

Fuck me. Forget pretending to be asleep—I'm going to pretend to be dead.

Wouldn't that be nice if she could. Instead, she had to be a grown-up about things.

"Hey, Ian. Alex is—" The word "here" devolved into a muffled "oof" as she turned and managed to smack her face into the wall of muscle that was Ian Petrov's chest. A delicious shiver worked its way through her—the kind that was a taste of out-of-control wildness she couldn't afford but damn her, she wanted to give in to it anyway.

"Yeah," he said, taking a step back and breaking contact

after he'd moved so silently to right behind her. "I see."

All right, she did not miss his touch—inadvertent or not—at all. Not a single bit.

Liar.

Annoyed at her own reaction, Shelby crossed her arms and matched him glare for glare. "Try not to make this completely awful. The guy did us a huge favor."

"Thanks for the lesson in manners." He kept his attention focused on the SUV outside. "I'll be sure to let my mom know what a shitty job she did with that."

She gasped and her cheeks flamed with embarrassment. That's not what she meant. Why did he always have to take everything as an attack? "There's no reason to go all total asshole with me."

"Well, we're heading back to reality, right?" He leveled a heated look at her. "Everything in the cabin was just the exception that proves the rule."

What should have been relief hurt too much to call it that. "Ian."

He shook his head. "Let's keep it to Petrov. Better yet, let's just keep it silent."

"You are a giant prick."

"You would know."

He smirked down at her, equal parts infuriating and addictive. Her temper, the one she kept on firm lockdown, flared to light. However, she was saved from committing murder in the lobby of the Buffly County Sheriff's Office by the massive guy with short, dirty-blond hair getting out on the SUV's driver's side and the one and only Lucy Kavanagh getting out from the passenger's side. She'd never been so glad to see someone so much in her life. Rushing out of the doors, she made an open-armed becline toward Lucy.

Wrapping her arms around the Ice Knights PR head, and technically her boss despite the firewall between marketing and the media hub, Shelby gave a grateful hug. "Thank you so much for coming."

"I've been freaking out since your message," Lucy said, returning the hug with a reassuring firmness. "I'm so sorry. The Airbnb said the cabin was a duplex, not just one building. I would never have done that to you had I known."

Shelby let loose a wry chuckle. "Well, if either of us had actually ended up at the right cabin, things may have been different."

"Right cabin?" Lucy's eyes rounded and she took a long gulp of her Mountain Dew. "What are you talking about?"

After she gave Lucy the short version—the one minus all the sexy naked parts—Lucy gave her another bone-cracking hug as Shelby looked over her shoulder at the two men ignoring each other with all the ferocity of two hockey players in the face-off circle in a triple-overtime game with the Stanley Cup on the line.

"Oh, wow. I'm surprised you're both still alive," Lucy said as she opened the SUV's back passenger-side door. "I'll sit in the back."

"I'll take the back and you can sit next to"—Ian cut his focus over to Alex—"him."

The other man let out a derisive huff of breath but didn't say anything.

Shelby shook her head. The two men may share only half their DNA, but it was obviously the stubborn and angry half.

"That works for me," Lucy said. "I have a lot to tell all three of you. I have a plan to fix all of" —she waved her hands around in the general direction of the others—"this."

Oh, great. Shelby's stomach sank. Whatever had happened while she and Ian were out of communication with the rest of the world, it must have been something.

"Nothing needs fixing," Ian said, each word coming out in a grumpy rumble. "I apologized to Shelby for mistakenly assuming that she leaked it all on purpose."

Lucy clapped her hands together and grinned at him like a proud mama. "You know what that is, Ian? Personal growth. Excellent. However, our troubles—the team's troubles—don't end there, do they? Lucky for you, I have a solution."

While Shelby was retreating into silence as guilt and dread swirled around inside her like a tornado of terribleness, the brothers didn't suffer the same problem. Both were grousing immediately.

"I'm not going into therapy," Alex said as he yanked open the driver's side door.

Ian narrowed his gaze in another of his signature glares. "Why do I think I'm not going to like whatever you're about to say."

"Because you're not *completely* brain dead," Alex said without ever looking over at his half brother. "Shocker."

"No one asked you, asshole." Ian tensed and puffed out his chest like a rooster about to go into full-tilt attack mode. "Shut your pie hole."

"Boys," Lucy said as she looked at Shelby and rolled her eyes in one of those woman-to-woman moments that needs no words. "You're probably both going to hate it, but if you want to keep your place on the team, you're going to do it. The word came down all the way from the owner's suite. This PR play is nonnegotiable, and it involves all three of you."

"Why me?" Shelby asked, shocked out of silence with her already squeaky voice going up to nails-on-a-chalkboard annoying even to her own ears.

"Because." Lucy bared her teeth in a smile that was anything but friendly. "The Biscuit as part of the Ice Knights media hub is the perfect place to tell the story of brothers reuniting on the road as they fight to win the Stanley Cup *together*."

Ian let out a string of mumbled curses before saying

clearly, "You've got to be kidding me."

Lucy turned to face him, her hands on her hips and her attitude just daring him to try it. "I'm not, and if any of you think of bucking the system here, it will not end well for you. You might rule on the ice, but I can scare the shit out of Godzilla without even breaking a sweat. You do not want to fuck with me." She gave Shelby, Ian, and Alex the stink eye and then jerked her head toward the SUV. "Now, everyone get in and I'll explain everything on the ride back to Harbor City."

• • •

The next two hours were already going to be absolute hell, but to add into it even the idea of getting all brotherly with Christensen—even if it was only for PR purposes—had Ian's gut churning. At least that made him forget the fact that he was sitting next to Shelby in an enclosed space.

Not that he was paying attention to that.

Or the way her black jeans clung to her long legs.

Or the way her cheeks got a little pink every time she looked at him, as if she couldn't stop thinking about last night, either.

Or the—

Fucking A, pull it together, man. She's not interested. Stop being such a rejection junkie.

"So here's how this is going to work," Lucy said as soon as they hit the interstate and a straight shot back to Harbor City. "Due to a freak glitch in the schedule, the Ice Knights have an extra-long road trip starting tomorrow."

"I thought I wasn't going on that because of this." He held up his busted thumb, which meant he still had about a week of off-ice time left.

"You can finish healing up on the road." Lucy shrugged.

"Plans change."

That static-electricity shock of oh-shit-he-was-not-going-to-like-this sizzled up the back of his neck. "So what's the new one?"

The smile on Lucy's face in response to his question would have scared the meanest goon in the league; it sure as hell had him prepping for a body blow.

"You two are going to room together on the road and you'll go to dinner together." Lucy turned her gaze on Shelby. "And our own intrepid correspondent from The Biscuit will be with you every step of the way to document and share with fans on the Ice Knights' social media hub."

It was an illegal hit to the head, and it stunned him into silence so solid that he would have sworn all his automatic bodily functions—his heartbeat, the ability to breathe, the little zaps of information from his brain that told his body how to work—stopped doing what they were supposed to and said, *To hell with it.*

"Fuck no," he and Christensen said at the same time.

"Oh look, you two are agreeing with each other already." Lucy clapped in sarcastic glee. "I'm overwhelmed by the power of this moment."

Everyone in the SUV fell silent after that. Ian's gaze met Christensen's in the rearview mirror and held for a moment before the other man looked away. Yeah, this was not going to work. Ever.

"How much coverage are you wanting?" Shelby asked, her quiet voice sounding resigned.

"Three to five posts a day," Lucy said. "This is going to be the bromance that takes the hockey world by storm, and we will control every moment of it."

Christensen scoffed. "People are going to see right through it."

"Then you two had better make it realer than real," Lucy

responded.

"Oh, come on," Ian said, unable to stop the bitter words from coming out. "You've been faking it for years; you should be a pro at it, Christensen."

The other man's grip on the steering wheel went white-knuckled. "I wasn't lying about a damn thing, Petrov."

Yeah, like he would ever believe that. "Whatever lies you have to tell yourself so you can sleep at night."

"Boys," Lucy cut in. "Stop glaring at me, Ian. I'm impervious, and it's just going to give you a headache. Don't smirk, Alex. You get in a wreck because of your speeding, and my husband will be the first firefighter here with the jaws of life to get you out just so he can beat you to a pulp. Understood?"

The SUV slowed perceptibly.

Ian couldn't blame Christensen for that. Lucy's husband, Frankie Hartigan, was the size of a small redwood tree with hands as big as baseball gloves. Hockey players never backed away from brawling, but taking on Hartigan wouldn't be a fight, it would be suicide—especially when it came to even maybe sorta having hurt Lucy. The man did not fuck around when it came to the woman he loved.

"All right, now that we're on the same page, I look forward to reading all the wonderful coverage on The Biscuit," Lucy said, her tone leaving no doubt that she didn't give a single solitary fuck if they agreed with her or not. This wasn't a her-way-or-the-highway. There was *only* Lucy's way. "Until then, I'm going to nap. The baby woke us up five times last night. If that kid ever learns to sleep through the night, I will never complain about anything ever again. Now, don't kill each other while I sleep. This shirt is one of the few I have without baby spit-up stains on it, and I don't want any blood splatter to ruin it."

There were rumors that Lucy had a softer side—and he'd

even seen it at her wedding when she was around her friends and family—but outside of that one time, he'd never witnessed it again. She was always in his top five scariest people he'd ever met in real life, and he played on the same line as Zach Blackburn, formerly the most hated man in Harbor City. Translation, Lucy was a take-no-shit badass.

Kind of like the other woman in the SUV.

He glanced over at Shelby. Her eyes were closed and her breathing steady, as if she'd followed Lucy's lead and had fallen asleep immediately, but he wasn't buying it. There was tension around those soft, way-too-kissable lips of hers that gave her away.

Fine. He could take a hint delivered with a two-by-four.

Out of habit, he opened his mouth to start shooting the shit with Christensen; then he realized what he was doing and closed it with enough force to make his teeth hurt. The two of them had spent every road trip debating which was the best Star Wars movie, busting chops about whomever the other was dating, and basically yammering about whatever popped into their heads nonstop until the plane landed or the bus arrived at the hotel. All of that was gone.

Good riddance.

Oh, he'd play nice with Shelby, who wanted to pretend that what had happened at the cabin hadn't actually happened. He'd fake being able to tolerate Christensen, who'd spent years lying about who he really was straight to Ian's face. However, that's all it would be. None of it would mean a damn thing.

He was better off without either of them.

Chapter Nine

Shelby woke up the next morning feeling like she hadn't just fallen off the wagon, she'd jumped gleefully into the abyss and ended up splattered on the concrete below—and she wanted to do it again, because a drink sounded like exactly the right way to take the edge off.

She'd heard about how amputees occasionally felt ghost limbs. For her, it was ghost hangovers. So even though she hadn't had a drink in six years, some days she woke up feeling as if she had and craving a little hair of the dog.

Lucky me.

Without getting out of bed, she took her six-year chip off the bedside table and flipped it over her fingers one at a time, going from pointer to pinkie and matching her inhales and exhales to the movement. In and out, slow and easy. The oxygen filled her lungs until her chest couldn't expand any more and then let it back out until that jagged urge for just one drink eased.

Unable to ignore the sun or the honks from the cars rushing in slow motion to merge onto the Harbor City Bridge just outside her apartment building anymore, Shelby got out of bed. She padded down the barely-big-enough-to-call-it-a-hallway to the galley kitchen, where an automatically brewed cup of heaven called coffee awaited her.

Her cell was in the charger next to the roll of paper towels and her apartment-size fridge covered in Ice Knights magnets. Needing to touch base with the most important man in her life before hitting the road, she pressed one of the four numbers in her phone contacts and poured her coffee while it rang.

"If it isn't my favorite Mustang," Roger said, his smile evident in his voice.

If there was one thing Roger Jones had always loved even more than Jim Beam, it was cars. However, he'd learned the hard way that the two didn't mix. One stint behind bars a few decades ago for his fifth DUI and his third trip to rehab finally changed that. He gave up the bourbon and kept the hot rods. When she'd told him her name was Shelby, yes like the classic muscle car, Roger had grinned up at her from his wheelchair and said they were a sponsor/sponsoree match made in automobile heaven.

"How's the V-8 running lately?" he asked.

"A little clunky."

"Meeting?"

There was no reason to specify what kind; she'd been going to AA meetings regularly since rehab. "Yeah, I'm going this morning at the church down the street before I have to pack and go on a road trip."

"Wait, aren't you on a trip now? Cabin? Middle of nowhere? Peace and quiet?"

More like anticipation and orgasms, frustration and satisfaction, annoyance and oh-my-God-fuck-yes. "That didn't work out quite like I'd expected."

"I can't wait to hear all about it. I gotta fresh cup of joe and the Charger for that Beckett billionaire can wait for a while."

That probably wasn't the case. The waiting list for the model hot rods Roger created in his studio seemed neverending thanks to an outsider art exhibit he'd been featured in at the Black Hearts Art Gallery. It was very Roger to make it sound like dropping everything to listen to her was no big deal, but still, she didn't want to take advantage.

"Are you sure?"

"Shelby," he said in that tone that made it impossible for her not to see the lines in his craggy face deepening as he frowned at her through the phone. "Don't act like I'm a pint of oil short. If I wasn't sure of it, I wouldn't have said it."

Since arguing with Roger was pointless, she told him everything. By the time she was done, her shoulders were a bit more relaxed, her coffee mug was empty, and that sharp poke of want that only a stiff drink could get rid of had been ground down to a nub.

"Girl," he said with a chuckle. "When you move, you really do go zero to sixty with things."

"And now I have to spend the entire road trip with him and his brother—whom he now hates."

It was going to be awful and amazing and uncomfortable and fun and a million other things that were a lot to take in all at once. Hell's bells. How in the world was she going to make it through this trip without losing her mind or her panties or both at the same damn time?

"Do you need to talk to that Lucy lady about backing out of the assignment?" Roger asked.

She'd be lying if she said she hadn't considered it. Last night, while she'd stared at her ceiling and worry turned into an all-you-can't-sleep buffet of anxiety, she'd definitely given it a lot of thought. But there was too much on the line. She'd worked her ass off for this opportunity. There was no way she'd fuck this up—no matter what.

"No. I can do this," she said, the affirmation coming out accompanied by that nervous-laughter thing she could never shake. Taking a deep breath, she centered herself. "I have to do this. This partnership with the Ice Knights is my dream outcome for The Biscuit. I can't let it get ruined because I was an idiot who slept with Ian Petrov."

She left the "and who wants to do it again and again and again" unsaid, but the truth of it had her fanning herself. Really, she was still sore in a few places she hadn't known existed.

"Lucky for you, I am available for the extremely low price of free, twenty-four hours a day, and I'll check out the Ice Knights road trip schedule and find a list of meetings you can go to on the road. I'll text it to ya later."

The offer made Shelby's throat clog with emotion. Screwing up her mouth and focusing on the ugly water stain on her ceiling to avoid tearing up, she took in a deep breath. Besides KiKi across the hall, Roger was one of the few people she could call a friend. That was something made all the more important, considering she was still trying to rebuild her relationship with her mom that she'd practically trampled into dust when she'd been drinking. The steps were well outlined in all the AA literature, but no one ever told a person how long they would take to complete them. Addiction gave no easy outs; it just felt like it did when she had been in the middle of a binge.

Now she knew different and, because of all she'd lost, every kindness in her life became a little sweeter. However, that didn't make it any easier to accept help.

"I can do that part," she said when she could finally get words out. "You don't have to."

"I want to," Roger said. "Anyway, I gotta admit I'm getting a real kick out of making that Richy Rich Beckett fella wait on me. Is that wrong?"

"Probably, considering he's your customer, but I'm not going to rat you out."

Roger laughed. "All right, girl, keep that engine of yours purring and reach out when you need me."

"Right back at you."

Feeling more settled than she had when she'd woken up, Shelby ended the call and put her coffee mug in the dishwasher. She walked across her tiny studio to the fish tank set up in front of the window looking across the harbor to the city and bent down to betta-fish level.

"Heya, Marvin. How you doin'?"

As was his custom, he ignored her and stayed turned toward the city. Yeah, her Waterbury apartment was small and overpriced, but the view was amazing. Seeing the sparkling city high-rises across the harbor's blue waters stole her breath every time. Some early mornings in the summer, she took her coffee and climbed out that very window to sit on the fire escape to watch all the commuter traffic crawl across the harbor bridge. Beyond her Hulu subscription, it was pretty much her only entertainment that didn't have to do with hockey.

Obsessed? Her? Hey, it could be worse. She could still be infatuated with bad bar pickups who never stayed the night and definitely never remembered her name.

She sprinkled some fish food into the tank, and that got Marvin's attention. He swam up and gobbled the flakes.

"Gird your loins, Marv. You're headed over to KiKi's later, where if you misbehave, she'll add you to whatever fancy event she's catering."

A flip of his fin and Marv moved to the other side of the tank, totally unbothered about becoming an hors d'oeuvres at a Harbor City society wedding. Smart fish. Bad attitude. He kinda reminded her of someone else who was surly as hell but pretty to look at. Well, she'd be seeing more than enough of him in the next few weeks.

Lucky me.

Letting out a groan, she headed for the shower to wash thoughts of that man right out of her head—as if that was possible.

. . .

Sweaty and breathing hard, Ian lay back on the yoga mat and cursed the online instructor who talked about practice and not perfection to a man who'd worked his whole life to get as close to perfect as possible—at least on the ice. That's where it mattered. That's where the world watched and judged.

Not that anyone was watching him. He wasn't allowed in the team gym until Doc had cleared him. All for a stupid thumb.

So here he was, getting his ass kicked by some dude named Sven who talked about the universe and releasing control and accepting yourself where you are. Well, Ian was in his living room, feeling like a moron for spending all of last night thinking about either Shelby or Christensen—but not at the same time, thank God. Those were two very opposite thought paths.

What he needed was that damn bottle of scotch he'd left at the cabin.

Sure it's not to fuck her again?

Shut up, brain.

They'd agreed. No repeats. No overtime. No more sex with Shelby.

Not your brain talking, Buck-O.

Obviously.

Great. Now he was talking to himself while using some of PopPop's favorite old-man words. Maybe it was a good thing he was getting out of the house for a while. Since the news about Christensen and him had broken, he'd pretty much gone into social isolation, and now he was having mental conversations with his dirty PopPop side. Isn't that what every grown man wanted to happen?

Fuck no. Time to stop feeling all boo-hoo for yourself.

Ian let out a long, deep breath before he responded to...himself...and for the first time in weeks was excited that his phone was ringing. He got up and grabbed it off the couch.

"Hey, Mom."

"So what's this I hear about you getting caught in the nasty late-season snow in some cabin and getting arrested?" Yep, that was Suzanne Petrov—straight, no chaser.

"It's nothing."

"Really?" He could practically see her eyebrow go up in tandem with her voice. "That's the kind of nothing a mother wants to know about her children."

"I am grown," he said as he walked down the hall to the oversize kitchen he pretty much never used.

She scoffed. "Did you grow so much, you stopped being my son?"

"No."

"Good." She paused just long enough to take half a breath. "So tell me everything, especially about this woman you were with. Is she someone special? Should I expect to meet her soon?"

Like that was going to happen. She wanted nothing to do with him. He was a trapped-in-a-cabin lay and that was it. Not that he cared what she thought. She was just some annoying kinda-reporter who stuck her nose where it didn't belong and then told the world—accidentally or on purpose.

"That is never going to happen." He grabbed an electrolyte-balanced water from the fridge and sucked a third of it down in one gulp while standing in front of the open fridge and letting the cool air hit him.

His mom *tsk-tsk*ed. "Such a sourpuss all of a sudden."

The ache in the back of his head, the one that throbbed and sizzled at the same time, went into overdrive at the reminder that his former good nature had died a sudden and painful death that hurt enough, it could have been written by George R. R. Martin. "I can't imagine why."

"Ian Elliot Petrov," his mom said, her tone sharp but with an edge of hurt. "I love you, but I've had just about enough of this attitude. I know you're hurt. I am, too. I'm also angry, confused, and a million other things. However, I'm not taking that out on you, and I expect you not to take it out on me."

She was right, but the person he wanted to take it out on, he couldn't even look at right now.

"Speaking of Dad, is he still calling you?"

"He is." She let out a soft sigh. "Not that you should be concerned about it. I'm taking care of it."

Ignoring the sharp edge of her tone, he dove right in to it like it was a bench-clearing brawl. "Of course I'm worried. You're my mom, and I don't want him to hurt you any more. I hate that he's done this to you."

"It's more complicated than that. It happened a long time ago. His cheating was definitely a reason for our split, but it wasn't the only one. Believe me, Ian, he's changed since then."

"People don't change." He crossed into his bedroom, passing by one of the many bookshelves in his apartment and the framed family photo that was not surprisingly missing dear old Dad. "Once someone picks their path, that's it."

He was proof of that. His path had been to prove the naysayers—especially his dad—wrong about his ability to make it to the NHL. And he'd done it. Next, he'd do what his dad couldn't and make his post-playing career mark in coaching. After that, there was just a big old blank spot, but who cared. He'd figure it out. Eventually.

"We all have more layers than that—even you," his mom said with a chuckle. "So what are you doing now?"

He stared down at the empty suitcase lying open in the middle of his bed, dread crawling up the back of his neck like a parade of ants wearing ice picks for shoes. "Packing for the team road trip."

"I thought you weren't going until after the doctor cleared you?"

"Change of plans." Yeah, that was one way to put it. As for him, he just called it Grade-A Bullshit. "The team wants to do a whole 'brothers bonding on the road' thing, and I'm stuck doing it."

"Oh, that's wonderful," his mom said without an ounce of sarcasm in her voice. "I think this is a great opportunity for you and Alex."

"Mom!" he exclaimed, almost dropping his phone. "How can you say that after what happened?"

"Because it wasn't his choice to be in this situation any more than it was yours."

The calm understanding in her voice was enough to push him right over the line. Heat blasted up through his body, setting every nerve ending on fire until he swore he could practically smell smoke.

"But. He. Lied," he said, slowly over-enunciating each word.

His mom made a *huh* sound. "Did he or did he not get lost in trying to figure out how to tell someone he cared about something that he knew would hurt him—sort of like how your father confessed to that affair and others when he thought coming clean could save our marriage but not to having another son."

How could his mother, the strongest woman he knew, come at him with questions like that? It made no sense.

"He lied." God, he hated how his voice broke on that last

word. "They both did."

"Ian, you are so stubborn sometimes that you remind me of your father."

"God forbid." There wasn't a damn thing of his father's that he wanted. Even if the hockey gods came down and offered to give him every one of his dad's on-ice skills, he'd turn them down flat.

Fuck David Petrov.

"I know you're mad," his mom said. "I was, too—for a very long time—but you know what I learned? It's not worth it. We are each the determiners of our own destiny, and I refuse to cede that power to someone who hurt me. That is *my* power. It's *yours*, too."

"I hate him." From the cowlick on the back of his head in the exact same spot as his dad's all the way down to the scar on Ian's ankle from the dog who bit him when he was five because his dad goaded him into petting the snarly poodle.

She let out one of those deep, soul-weary Mom sighs that seemed to go on forever. "Well, I love you."

"I love you, too."

"Take a deep breath and give Alex a chance. We're all trying to do our best in this world and making the best decisions we can at the time with the information we have."

If he was 10 percent as good of a person as his mom was, he'd take her advice. But he really was too much his father's son. The truth of it made him sick to his stomach, but there it was.

"Bye, Mom."

He hung up and tossed his phone down on the bed. It landed with a soft *thump* next to his empty suitcase. How in the hell was he going to make it two weeks with Shelby? Alex he could ignore—or at least seem to. There was no pretending he could not notice Shelby.

"You are so fucked, Petrov."

Chapter Ten

In the past, Ian looked for one thing when it came to finding a seat on the team charter jet—Christensen's big head. If he didn't see him, he'd definitely hear him because the guy never shut up. It was one of the things they had in common—big mouths always running at full speed.

This time, however, Ian climbed the jetway stairs and kept his gaze aimed at armrest level, hoping to spot an empty row that he could park in and snarl at anyone who tried to sit next to him. He made it three steps down the aisle before Lucy got up from her seat and blocked his path forward. She had dark bags under her eyes and her ten-month-old on one hip.

"Here, take Freya," she said as she held the baby out to him.

Ian didn't mean to take the baby. It just sort of happened. It was like seeing a flash of a defender's jersey in his peripheral and bracing for a hit; he just let instinct take over. Of course that didn't mean he had any idea what he was doing. As he held the kid out at arm's length, she eyed him warily.

Back at you, Small Fry.

Lucy picked up her purse from the seat she'd gotten out of. "You and Alex have plane duty. Frankie was on shift yesterday, so that meant it was all me getting up four billion times last night. I swear whoever came up with the idea of twenty-four-hour shifts for firefighters should be made to march to the edge of a cliff and shoved off. I'd do it myself, but I'm too damn tired."

Ian looked back at the kid. Freya had a mop of red hair, freckles scattered all across the chubby cheeks that grandmothers liked to pinch, and a glint in her eyes that reminded him way too much of her formidable mom. She didn't look like a non-sleeping demon, but what in the hell did he know about kids?

"Why did you give me your baby?" he asked.

Lucy let out a weary sigh. "Because I'm exhausted and need a nap. Don't worry, this little fluff muffin has been fed and should sack out after takeoff." She lifted up the pacifier attached to Freya by a length of ribbon decorated with hockey pucks. "Here's a binky in case her ears bother her. You and Alex can swap off holding her."

"Why would I—"

And that's when he finally looked over at the set of seats next to Lucy's. It was one of the two sets of four seats that sat facing each other, two on two, that were usually reserved for the team captain. Christensen sat in one chair closest to the window, his body tense as he looked out of the jet. Across from him sat Shelby, dressed all in black with an aggressive electric-blue line sailing across her top eyelids and ending in a little swoop shape that reminded him of wings. She took one look at him, straightened her shoulders, and let out a deep breath as if she'd spent the past sixty years prepping for this moment with absolute dread.

Forget awful, this situation was a fucking nightmare. He

was stuck on a plane holding a baby—*a baby!*—he'd never seen before, while sitting next to his former best friend whom he wasn't speaking to and across from the woman he had the hots for—*thanks, PopPop, for giving me the mental slang of a Boomer*—who would rather never set eyes on him again. Even worse? They were all forced to stay together like this for the entirety of a cross-country flight that would last approximately six hundred years.

Ian slid his gaze back over to Lucy. "You've got to be kidding me."

"I never joke when it comes to my sweet Freya." She blew a kiss to the baby, who was drooling like someone had left a tap on. "She gets grumpy right before she falls asleep. I suggest tucking her in against you and letting her stroke your hair. It seems to calm her down the fastest."

With that, the team's PR genius and his personal tormentor walked down the aisle to the back of the plane, sat down in an empty row, popped in her earphones, and closed her eyes.

Meanwhile, he was still standing in the middle of the aisle, blocking the handful of Ice Knights players trying to get to their seats—the lucky kind that didn't come with a baby, a nemesis, or the woman who had told him to go straight to the penalty box and not come back. The baby wiggled in his grip, her little chin starting to tremble under the weight of her apparent dissatisfaction. His pulse picked up and his mind went blank. This was like holding a live bomb, and he had no idea which wires to cut.

He looked over at Christensen and Shelby. Christensen still sat with his back to the aisle. Shelby just lifted an eyebrow and shook her head. Panic starting to make his palms sweat, Ian adjusted his hold on Freya but kept his arms locked so she was about as far away from him as possible.

Squaring his jaw, he gave the baby a firm look. "You're

not gonna cry."

Freya's answer was to let out an earsplitting yowl and turn a shade of purple he hadn't been aware was possible for a human. Grown men winced. Stuckey, who was known for slamming into people with enough force to knock teeth out, sank down into his seat as if to hide. He swore he spotted Lucy smirking for half a second before she flattened her lips and went back to pretend sleeping.

"You can't hold a baby like that if you want her not to cry," Christensen said, his voice having no problem cresting over the crying.

Turning to Christensen, he glared at the other man. "How do you know?"

The forward's's expression turned smug. "Because I babysat all through high school to pay for my hockey gear."

"So take her." He held the baby out to Christiansen.

Freya hollered louder.

"No way." He held up his hands, palms forward. "Lucy said you had first shift."

Freya wailed again. It was like an ice pick being jabbed into his ear. Ian turned to Shelby and silently offered her the kid.

Her blue-lined eyes rounded before narrowing into tiny slits. "Why, because I'm a woman?"

Ian didn't respond. She looked like a woman who knew how to fillet a man and was getting ready to show off her skills on him—probably with a rusty knife that had a dull edge.

The sound of a fake cough that distinctly sounded like "dumbass" came from the direction of Christensen, but Ian's gaze was locked on Shelby. It wasn't that he couldn't stop staring because he really thought she'd shiv him, but that he just couldn't look away. Steel and softness wrapped up in a fuck-you package complete with leather boots and a vine tattoo he'd kissed from one thorn to the next, Shelby was turning into his fucking catnip.

Too bad she wanted absolutely nothing to do with him, as she'd made plain at the sheriff's office. The reminder had his gut twisting, and he pulled Freya in closer until her soft hair tickled his chin and she snuggled into his shoulder. Why did he do it? Because he remembered Lucy's advice or because he needed a hug? Fuck if he knew, but the toddler's chubby little fingers that no doubt were sticky with kid goobers immediately sought out his hair.

"Please take your seats, Ice Knights," the pilot said over the intercom. "It's time to get this bird in the air."

Ian looked from the empty seat by Christensen to the one next to Shelby. There was no good choice here, but he had to make it. The devil he could ignore or the devil who made him feel like some sad-sack sucker who wanted what he couldn't ever have? Oh yeah, that last bit sounded familiar.

Ian sat down next to Christensen and tried not to grimace as Freya went from petting his hair to straight-up trying to yank it out of his head as she sucked her thumb.

"Your turn soon, Christensen," he said, as if that was why he'd picked that seat rather than the one next to Shelby.

"Works for me." The other man shrugged and turned back to the window. "Babies love me."

Of course they did. Everyone loved Alex Christensen. It was hard not to like him unless you had a massively important reason—which Ian sure as hell did.

He did the awkward moves necessary to buckle his seat belt while holding a crashed-out kid. Finally finished with the sixteen-part play, he looked up and right at Shelby. The team jet was already zooming down the runway when he realized his mistake. He'd have to spend the entire flight across the country staring right at the woman he hadn't been able to get out of his head since she jabbed that Taser of hers into his ribs.

Just great.

• • •

Shelby had no interest in having kids anytime soon. Babies did nothing for her. Her ovaries did not explode when a photo of a hot guy holding a baby crossed her social media streams. She didn't sigh and press her hand to her heart when she spotted teeny-tiny booties. The sound of an infant giggling didn't make her want to toss her pills in the trash.

So why in the hell couldn't she stop staring at Ian as Freya snuggled deeper agains his chest and drooled on his crisp white dress shirt? Why did it do funny things to her stomach? And why in the name of Gordie Howe did it make her all melty?

It wasn't just the fact that his shoulders seemed broader or his hands bigger or that—

"Wanna switch seats?" Alex asked.

The question jarred her out of the hot-guy-with-a-baby trance she'd accidentally landed in and she startled, trying—and failing—to appear cool about it. "No. Why would I want to do that?"

The Ice Knights' other first-line forward grimaced. "Because the things I'm reading on your face as you stare at him are making me uncomfortable."

So much for not making an idiot of herself on her first official workday. Great. Fabulous. Wonderful. Why didn't they give out parachutes when a person boarded just in case of extreme in-flight-embarrassment events like this?

"Stop making shit up to bust her chops," Ian said, keeping his gaze focused on the empty chair in front of him as if it held the secret to winning the lotto.

"He speaks to me." Alex let out a dramatic gasp. "Careful there, or between calling me when you used your get-out-of-jail-free card and addressing me directly, people might think you'd actually pulled your head out of your ass."

Ian barely unclenched his jaw as he responded. "There is a baby here."

"Freya isn't going to repeat it."

Even with the undeniable tension between Alex and Ian, there was something else, too—a connection that only really good friends or siblings had.

It made all of this back-and-forth idiocy tolerable because as an only child, Shelby had never experienced it. She'd only watched longingly as her friends fought with their brothers and sisters one minute and then zoomed into protector mode the next. What would that be like to have someone so firmly on your side? Ian and Alex were both morons for not seeing how lucky they were.

"Yeah, so you say." Ian snorted, then went completely still when the baby wiggled around in his arms. The second she settled back in with a soft sigh and closed her eyes again, Ian kept his voice low. "Wait until Lucy comes after you because Freya's first word is 'ass.'"

"I'll tell her you said it while holding Freya. It's true. You just did. And *you*"—Alex turned his focus onto her, pulling her into the discussion from the sidelines—"were staring at him like you were ready to take a bite out of him—in the good way."

"You're mistaken." There, that almost came out as if she wasn't lustily remembering every touch, every stroke, every kiss that had happened between them.

Alex lifted an eyebrow. "Am I?"

Ian's gaze locked with hers and her breath caught. There was just something in the look in his eyes, the demand and the promise, that had her entire body humming with need. This was bad. This was so very, very bad. And she'd never wanted anything more. The reaction was so outsized, so out of character that the shock of it was a bucket of ice water tossed onto the fire that always seemed to sizzle to life around Ian.

"So you two got stuck in that cabin together for a week?" Alex asked, his voice sounding distant.

Unable to look away from Ian, she replied, "Three days."

"Uh-huh. And the cabin lost power?"

"Yeah," Ian said, the word coming out more like one of his sexy cabin grunts than English.

"Had to find a way to stay warm, huh?"

She flushed. "There was a fireplace."

One that was warm enough to lie in front of naked for hours. Or was that because of Ian? Damn. She was scared the answer was the second one.

"Any chance there was a bear rug in front of it?" Alex looked from her to Ian, his grin getting bigger with each second. "I see."

"You see nothing," Ian said, his tone as harsh as his hold on Freya was gentle.

"You're right," Alex said. "It's not at all what I was thinking. You two. Alone. A cabin. Sex pheromones flying through the air, rubbing up against each other."

"Nothing happened," Shelby said, surprised she wasn't hit by a lightning bolt on the spot for that lie.

"Then maybe it should have," Alex said. "Unleashing all this pent-up attraction upon unsuspecting folks like myself in the middle of a tin can shooting through the sky seems a mite dangerous."

"You're imagining things," Ian said.

God knew she was right now, and pretty much all of them involved being naked.

"I am?" Alex laughed. "Fine. Whatever you two say. I won't say another word about it."

With that, the other man crossed his arms over his navy dress shirt, leaned his head against the headrest, and closed his eyes.

Relief swept through Shelby from her boots up her pleather pants to the dressy top she'd ironed this morning so she'd fit in with Coach's requirement that everyone dress up during road trips to the tips of her multi-pierced ears. The last thing she needed now that she was officially on the job was to have someone figure out that she and Ian had had sex. On a bearskin rug. In front of a roaring fire.

Oh God. She was a hot mess, and she could only think of one way to make it through this cross-country flight. She closed her eyes and pretended to fall asleep. Immediately. She considered fake snoring but decided against it.

Hours later, when the captain announced they were landing, she opened her eyes and did a fake stretch, as if she hadn't spent the entire flight with her ears attuned to Ian's every shift in his seat. Not that anyone would know that. Against her better judgment, she snuck a peek at Ian. He was still holding Freya, but he was looking right at Shelby.

One side of his mouth curled up in a smirk that all but screamed that she wasn't fooling anyone.

Way to go, Shelby. They obviously should be meeting the plane to give you your Oscar.

So even though she knew he knew, and he no doubt knew that she knew he knew, they both kept their mouths shut on the team bus to the hotel. She ditched him in the hotel lobby, making a quick break for the shortest check-in line. However, her hotel luck turned out to be the same as her grocery store luck, and she picked the line that barely moved. Once she finally had her room key in hand, Ian was nowhere to be seen. Sending up a quick thank-you to the fates, she hustled to the hotel elevator so she could hide in her room.

Chicken? Me? Cluck, cluck.

She stepped inside the crowded elevator just as the doors were closing. And it wasn't until the mirrored doors shut that she realized Ian was in the back of the elevator car. At the opposite corner stood Alex. Heart hammering in her chest, she glued her gaze to the numbers lighting up on the elevator panel. With each stop, the elevator emptied out a little, but Ian and Alex remained. It wasn't until they hit the twentieth floor—her floor—that all three of them got off.

Alex took one look from her to his brother and back again before rolling his eyes. "Yeah, absolutely no unfinished business between you two at all." Then he shook his head and headed down the hall.

Ian answered with a noncommital grunt that sent her straight back to the cabin. Her skin flushed all of a sudden, and she kept her gaze on the room numbers and not the hot hunk of man next to her. They stopped at the same time.

Not again.

He jerked his head to the door opposite hers. "This is me."

"I'm right here." Was that relief making her stomach sink? Yes. Had to be. There was no way it was disappointment.

He nodded and headed for his door, rubbing the back of his neck. After swiping his key card and turning the knob, he paused. "I'll see you for dinner, then."

"Yeah," she said, her mutinous body perking up in inconvenient places. *Not a date, boobs, it's work.* "You and Alex get to have brotherly bonding that I'll tell the world about."

He grimaced before striding into his room and letting his door swing shut.

Way to go, Shelby. You are so a people person. Always with the right thing to say.

Letting out a sigh, she went into her own room so could shower off the flight and maybe—just maybe— head on straight before she had to spend the ev a hot, surly hockey player she absolutely for

nothing to do with beyond a professional work relationship.
 Really.
 For sure.
 Without even an itty-bitty smidgen of doubt.

Chapter Eleven

An hour later, Ian walked into the private room of the hotel's restaurant to find he was the last to arrive. Everyone else was already at the table, enjoying appetizers and gabbing about the Phoenix players they'd be facing off against tomorrow.

Normally, he'd be all on board for some pregame smack talk, but that would be all it would be for him because of his stupid thumb injury. He wasn't even wearing a brace anymore, just some wimpy little bandages that declared what a dumbass he was for tripping over his own big feet. It barely hurt anymore; he had range of motion back—okay, mostly back. All he had to do was talk Doc into giving him the okay.

How hard could that be?

Spotting the free seat by the team doc, Ian made his way over to the table. It had to be a sign from above. This was gonna happen. He was getting back on the ice, and then that nagging sense of not being enough would shut the fuck up.

"Heya, Doc." Ian pulled out the empty chair. "Anyone sitting here?"

Doc, an older guy with not even a hint of hair on his

perfectly round pale-pink head, looked up at him. "Not you, I'm afraid."

What the hell? How had he turned an affable guy like Doc against him?

Before he could ask, Lucy walked up with Freya in her arms. The chubby little baby gave him a huge gummy smile, showing off one tooth starting to come in.

"What Doc means is that your reservation is for that table over there." Lucy pointed to a three-person table in the corner.

One that Christensen and Shelby were already sitting at. Shelby was listening to whatever bullshit story Christensen was telling her with utter rapt attention, a soft smile crinkling the corners of her eyes. Ian was grinding his molars together before he even took the first step toward them.

Christensen was like this with every woman. It had barely registered with Ian until now—until Shelby. Gaze locked on Shelby, the way her lips had curled into a half smile as if Christensen was the most fascinating person ever, he marched past the long table of Ice Knights players who weren't in PR hell.

"Have fun at the little kids' table, Petrov," said Stuckey, a defenseman who was a constant smart-ass when he wasn't on the phone with his girlfriend or telling the team stories about the horse of a Great Dane they shared.

"Are you ever going to stop being in a shit-ass mood?" asked Phillips, the team Thor look-alike.

"Not until I'm on the ice," he shot back as he strode past, barely slowing in his speed as he watched Shelby lean in closer to Christensen to take a look at whatever it was he was showing her on his phone.

"Have pity on us, Doc," the team captain, Zach Blackburn, hollered from his place at the head of the big table. "Clear the asshole."

"Don't drag me into this, boys," Doc said. "The body heals when it heals. You can't hurry it."

Doc took a deep breath that was no doubt the precursor to a mini lecture on patience, visualization, and doing what it took to stay healthy, which Ian considered his cue to speed the fuck up before he got called in to be used as an example of exactly what not to do. He'd heard the speech before, and that was more than enough.

He had no more than sat down at the tiny circular table when a waiter came by with two large glasses of milk over ice and put one down in front of Christensen and the other in front of him.

Finally, something was going right today. Ian let out a sigh of relief and the muscles in his shoulders unwound enough to inch downward from his earlobes.

Shelby wrinkled her nose. "Milk? Really?"

"It does a body good," he and Christensen said at the same time.

Ian was grinning and holding up his glass to clink against Christensen's before he realized it. He stopped just in time, changing direction so he gulped down half his milk in one swallow instead.

It was habit—everyone on the team busted their chops about the milk. It had just made them more likely to order it more often until it became part of their pregame routine. Fine. Superstition. There was no shame in that. Hockey players were notorious for being very specific when it came to game prep. Stuckey had been wrapping his stick the same way since Juniors at least. Blackburn isolated, scaring the shit out of anyone who broke his silent zone. He and Christensen drank milk and chipped at each other. It was what worked. No one fucked with that, not even when the other guy was a complete asshole.

"I went through two gallons a week growing up."

Christensen wiped a milk mustache away with the back of his hand.

Like that was anything to brag about. "Me too."

"Maybe it was three," Christensen said.

Ian snorted. "Oh yeah, well—"

Shelby interrupted with an exhausted sigh. "If you two don't stop now, one of you will have grown up drinking straight from the cow until it was sucked dry."

The mental picture she described would be giving him nightmares for the next sixty years.

Christensen made a gagging sound. "Gross, Shelbs."

Annoyance sharp as a poker jabbed Ian in the right eyeball. "Shelbs?"

The fuck? They were becoming buddies with pet names for each other? After spending ten minutes together at this stupid table with its white tablecloth and little candle sitting in the middle?

"That's her nickname." Christensen shrugged. "Everyone needs a nickname. I'm The Smile and you're—"

"David Petrov's journeyman son," Ian finished, the bitterness in those four words etched into the marrow of his bones.

That's all he was to most people—the not-quite-as-good substitute. And now the second-place son. He didn't have to wonder what they thought. Everyone was always more than glad to share it in every sports column, blog, and Instagram comment.

Christensen picked up his glass. "Our dad is an asshole."

He didn't think, didn't consider. The words were just too true for that. "On that we can agree." He clinked his glass against Christensen's.

They both chugged the rest of their milk at the same time—another tradition—while Shelby watched them from across the table as if she was trying to decipher hieroglyphs.

"Is this the beginning of a truce?"

Ian glared at his his former best friend. "Not even close."

"Too bad." She took a sip of her water with lemon. "You two are the only people in the world who know what it's like to be David Petrov's son. Man, I'd give anything to have a brother or sister."

Yeah, maybe if their father hadn't hidden Christensen's existence for all of Ian's life and then if his former best friend hadn't continued to keep their dad's secret when he'd known the truth the entire time, things would be different. But they weren't. His dad and Christensen had both shown their true colors.

"This situation is a little different than the usual," he said.

"True." Shelby picked up her menu. "But you two are pretty far from the usual, too."

Before he could come up with a retort about how wrong Shelby was, the waiter showed up to take their orders and he was left to wonder if she just might be right.

• • •

For two solid days, Shelby had done everything she could to make sure she wasn't alone with Ian. It sounded easy when she'd made the plan in her head. Of course, that was before she realized that he'd be sitting in the visitor's suite watching the Ice Knights games with her.

Lucy had taken pity on her and joined them for the Phoenix game, but tonight in L.A., Freya had let it be known in no uncertain terms that she wasn't up for sitting through another game.

"I'll watch from my hotel room," Lucy said as she headed for the suite's door. "Don't do anything stupid while I'm too far away to give you the evil eye."

Now it was just the two of them. And he was in a suit.

She'd always been a sucker for a guy in a good suit. Ian's had probably been custom-made. That would explain how it fit his broad shoulders perfectly and clung to his high, round hockey ass like it had been made for him—because it had.

Look away, Shelby. There be dragons with really great asses.

Ian glanced over at her and narrowed his eyes. "Why are you looking at me like that?"

"Like what?" she all but squeaked in response as she took her seat as quickly as possible and became incredibly fascinated by the linesmen doing their warm-up circles around the ice.

He let out a grunt. "With your nose all wrinkled like I stink."

Ian did smell. *Wonderfully.* So much so that she may have leaned closer while they were getting drinks from the buffet at the back of the suite so she could get a good long whiff. God, if he noticed that, she was going to die of embarrassment right here.

"Is that why you smelled me before?" He sat down next to her and did one of those sly pit-sniffing maneuvers.

Fuck. Fuck. Fuckity fuck fuck. "I was clearing my sinuses."

One eyebrow went up. One yeah-sure grunt was emmited. One very hot hockey player turned away from her and focused back on the ice below where his teammates were lined up for the first face-off of the game. Meanwhile, Shelby sat there frozen with indecision about whether to go all in and tell him about her myriad sinus issues and the fact that she knew absolutely nothing about her fake ailment.

The hockey gods, though, took pity on her.

The puck hit the ice and they were both glued to the action. Pheonix wasn't a dirty team like the hated Cajun Rage, but they were hard-hitting, take-no-prisoners go-getters and they wanted to win. Badly.

By the end of the first period, Shelby's voice had gone hoarse from yelling. By the end of the second, she'd thrown off any pretense of maybe-sorta-kinda playing it cool and had spent most of it either standing up and cheering on the Ice Knights or pacing in front of the buffet table, grumbling about missed passes as she rolled her six-year-sober coin over her knuckles like the talisman it had become. By the time the second intermission started, she was twisted up so tight, she was ready to pop.

Plate of snacks in one hand and an unopened beer in the other, Ian sent a pitying look her way. "Want a beer?"

She palmed her six-year chip, her attention yanked away from the possibilities of the third period. "Nah."

"Want something else?" He glanced back at the well-stocked bar behind the buffet table. "This place has pretty much everything."

"Ginger ale, please."

It was her go-to. Carry around a glass of that and people assumed it was spiked. It wasn't that she was hiding her sobriety but more that she dreaded having to deal with the other person's reaction. It usually fell into one of three categories. One, pity. Two, scorn. Three, the come-on-you-don't-look-like-an-alcoholic-just-have-one-drink disbelief.

Ian nodded and grabbed an old-fashioned glass. "With?"

She let out a small sigh and braced for the conversation she'd been hoping to avoid. "Ice."

He hesitated for half a second and swiveled around to face her. "You don't drink?"

And there it was. Her gut knotted in anticipation of how he'd react. It shouldn't matter—she barely knew Ian—but somehow it did.

The reality of that fact had her lifting her chin in defiance as she looked him straight in the eye, ready to take the metaphorical hit. "Not anymore."

It was easy to spot the moment the lightbulb went off. The slight wrinkling of his forehead and the quick nod. "Sorry."

No pity. No scorn. Definitely no come-get-drunk-anyway disbelief. It was more of just straight acceptance.

Ian handed her the ginger ale. "How long?"

"Six years."

He took a bite off a carrot stick and shot her a long, contemplative look while he crunched. "And how long has The Biscuit been around? It's been about that, hasn't it?"

"Yeah, close to six years." Yeah, that brain of his put that together quick. But that had to mean— She gasped. "Are you a secret reader?"

"Maybe." The tips of his ears turned pink, and he hustled back toward their seats.

What? That couldn't be. She knew her stats. Most of her visitors engaged; that's what made her site special enough to gain the Ice Knights' attention, which meant…

She hurried as fast as she could with a ginger ale filled nearly to the brim down the five stadium steps to the suite's private row of seats and sat down next to Ian. "Have you commented?"

He snapped another carrot in half with one bite and ignored her.

Oh no, this wasn't going away that easily. No. Way. She cleared her throat with a dramatic "ahem."

Letting out a long-suffering sigh, he kept his gaze on the ice as the final period started. "I have not commented as myself."

The puck dropped. The clock started. The play went on. And Shelby couldn't stop staring at the man who'd followed her blog when he had a million other things he could have been doing with his time. "Aren't you just an onion."

"As long as I don't smell like one," he shot back.

The urge to tease him about following The Biscuit was there, but she wasn't going to keep poking at the bear's vulnerable underbelly. They could have an unstated truce again. It was better than the pretending each other didn't exist, especially since her job basically depended on being around him nearly twenty-four-seven.

"So who do you think is going to finally score?" she asked during a break in play. "My money's on Alex."

Ian scoffed. "Nope. He's got the twitch tonight. Not gonna happen."

She zeroed in on Alex as he sat on the bench fiddling with his stick as he watched a replay on the Jumbotron. "The twitch?"

"Watch the way he can't sit still." Ian nodded at his half brother, a knowing grin on his face, as if he'd had this conversation with Alex a time or twenty. "He's messing with the tape on his stick, he's asking for gloves that have been sitting on the heater in the tunnel, he's chewing on his mouth guard like it's bubble gum. He's shit-talking himself in his head after that missed pass. That play always gets him in his own brain. He won't score. What he needs is to refocus and work on that play until it's muscle memory."

"So help him fix it, Coach Know-It-All."

He grunted and retreated back into himself as the players took the ice and the game resumed.

In the end, it was Phillips who scored off a beauty of a slap shot that the goalie never saw coming. It was one of the most gorgeous things she'd ever see. Shelby jumped out of her seat, yelling her head off. High off the thrill of a close victory, she spun around to face Ian, right hand raised for a high five. Instead of slapping his hand against hers, though, he wound his arms around her waist, picked her up, and twirled her. She didn't think; she just threw her arms around his neck and kissed him with maybe—okay totally with—a little bit of tongue. In that moment, with her entire body zoned in only on Ian, the feel of him pressed against her, she forgot the crowd and the game and the rest of the world. Then he broke the kiss and she remembered where she was, who he was, and exactly why this was a very bad idea.

"Shit." She pushed softly against his shoulders and he let her down. The second her feet hit the ground, she wanted to run. "I'm sorry. That was wrong of me. I shouldn't have done that. Very unprofessional."

He rubbed the back of his neck and turned toward the ice. "It was a good goal."

"Really good," she said, trying to ignore the way her lips were still tingling and how that feeling had zipped all the way to her core.

"Amazing," he said, looking everywhere but at her. "One for the highlights."

Oh God, this wasn't awkward at all. "Without a doubt."

At least this road trip couldn't get any worse.

• • •

Ian hadn't stopped thinking about that kiss in two days.

Every meal when he, Christensen, and Shelby had been sequestered from the team on Lucy's PR orders for "bonding time," he'd talked, but he'd been wondering if she kept remembering that kiss, too. Every time they had to watch a game with an empty seat between them like a personal DMZ, he couldn't help but curse a little extra that the team had entered a scoring drought. And now, when she was across the practice rink in Vancouver as the team practiced drills and he did a slow skate around the oval, finally cleared by the doc for that much at least, he still couldn't stop thinking about it.

Yeah, he was watching her as she sat on the bench yakking with Christensen whenever he stopped nearby.

He had no clue what they were talking about, but it must have been funny as hell considering the size of her smile. Meanwhile, Ian was doing loops around the ice like it was couple skate and he was the lone loser out by himself.

"Ian," Shelby hollered, waving him over.

His gut reaction was to ignore her, because God knew he'd been practicing that for the past few days. However, her shout had cut through the sounds of the skates and sticks, and every player on the team glanced over at him. Then they all stopped, their blades turning the ice to snow as they skidded to a stop. Gossipy assholes, they just wanted to see what would happen next.

Of course, if this didn't involve him, he'd be gawking without shame, too.

There really wasn't a way to avoid being a damn coffee klatch, always in one another's business when you spent nine months out of the year skate-to-skate with one another.

Since there was no way around it, he made his way over to the bench. It took everything he had not to land a not-so-friendly hip check on the other man for talking to Shelby with that hey-baby smirk of his that had landed him on billboards with millions in endorsement deals. That, of course, made no sense. There were a billion other reasons to put the weight down on Christensen, but flirting with Shelby? What the hell did he care?

"So Alex here"—Shelby smiled at Christensen as if he were hot chocolate on an icy morning—"doesn't think he has tells when he's mad at himself during a game."

"Are you kidding?" Christensen asked with a chuckle. "I'm always cool."

Ian laughed. Out loud. A huge belly laugh that made his abs ache.

Christensen's jaw squared, and his eyes narrowed. "Fine. What's my tell?"

"There are about a billion of them." He flicked the top of the other man's stick. "If you don't stop messing with the tape after you miss passes, the other teams are going to notice, and then the Rage are going to tear you apart."

The Ice Knights' biggest rivalry games were always preceded by hours of watching film of the other team to gain any edge—no matter how small—to take the other team out. There was no way the players on the Cajun Rage weren't doing the same thing.

"It's a new play," Christensen said.

"So practice." Until every move was like breathing.

Christensen scoffed. "What, you're ready to show me how it's done?"

More than ready. Watching the games from the visitor's suite was torture. "Let's do it."

He'd been on the ice with Christensen running the passing drill under Coach's watchful eye for close to thirty minutes before he realized Shelby wasn't there anymore. One moment she'd been on the bench watching them, and the next time he looked over, she was gone. If he didn't know any better, he'd think she'd set up this little "brotherly" practice session.

Christiensen came to a fast stop next to him, the edge of his skates sending snow-cone-thin layers of ice flying. "You know she did."

Had he said it out loud? Was he finally losing it? Nah. There's no way. "What are you talking about?"

"I can still read you like an unlocked phone. She totally made this happen right after she was telling me what a great coach you'd be."

Fuck. Was he that easy to maneuver? "You're both a pain in my ass."

"You're not wrong, but she's right, too. You are a pretty good coach." Christensen looked away, down toward the empty goal. "I've been working on the play for weeks. This is the first time it felt right." He cleared his throat and started toward the tunnel leading to the locker room. "Thanks, Petrov."

"Anytime," he shot after him, taken aback when he realized he meant it.

What if his mom was right? Maybe Christensen did have a side to this story. A very feminine laugh yanked his attention away from that unpleasant thought. Shelby was back, this time chatting with Lucy in the stands. He couldn't have looked away if he'd been run over by the Zamboni.

Because he was staring, he was looking right at her when she tried to sneak a peek at him, her cheeks going pink the moment she realized she'd gotten caught. Her fingers went immediately to her lips, as if she couldn't stop thinking about that kiss, either.

Makes two of us, sweetheart. So what are we going to do about it?

Chapter Twelve

Shelby was going to hyperventilate and pass out alone, all because of one stupid headline and an out-of-context pic. She wasn't even out of her softest cotton nightgown and hadn't started the hotel room coffee maker, but she was 100 percent fully awake at the ungodly hour of six a.m. thanks to her social media notifications going on a buzzing spree. Ignoring the sound would have been the best plan. Then again, so would sticking to her original plan of not lusting after one Ian Petrov. That hadn't worked out, either.

So in a move that would surprise absolutely no one, she'd looked.

Secret Brothers Share More Than Just Their Famous Hockey Dad?

Underneath the headline on the sleaziest hockey gossip site on the entire internet was a photo of Ian, Alex, and her in Chicago last night. She had no idea what they'd been talking about when the picture had been taken, but at first glance it definitely looked like there was more to last night's dinner than just deep dish. It was cropped so the viewer couldn't see the other table with the rest of the team sitting at it. Also, the angle was shooting downward so it looked like the V-neck of her shirt went deeper than it did. And whatever filter or magic the photographer had used to make it look like Ian was gazing adoringly at her as Alex refilled her water glass without a doubt made it seem as if they were at an intimate dinner for three.

Just when she thought it couldn't get worse, she made the mistake of reading the article. There was every single double entendre connected to hockey possible, a deep dive into the rumors of a rivalry between Ian and Alex since it became public knowledge that they shared a dad, and for the cherry on the puke-flavored ice-cream sundae, there was a quote from someone who'd been at rehab with her noting that she'd turned to hockey when she gave up the bottle.

Making the supremely smart move to back away from the internet before she scrolled down and read the comments, Shelby turned her phone over and laid it on the hotel pillow. It sat there like a speck of blue in the sea of cream that was the hotel's expansive, downy comforter, calling out to her like a siren. Even knowing that finding out what was in the comments would be akin to smashing her head against the rocks, the temptation had her twitchy.

How bad could it be?

People were generally skeptical of salacious gossip, right?

What if the commenters would give her the benefit of the doubt as opposed to calling her a slut like some kind of misogynistic reflexive action?

What would it hurt to take one quick look to gauge the reaction?

She picked up the phone, but the unexpected sound of someone banging on her door when it was still o'dark hundred shocked a yelp right out of her and she dropped her cell back down on the pillow.

"Shelby," Ian said through the door, sounding barely awake himself. "Let me in."

She squeezed her eyes shut and went bunny-hears-a-noise still. No doubt he was here to yell at her, probably assuming that she'd tipped off the tabloid photographer just like he'd figured she'd leaked the story about Alex being his brother. Maybe he hadn't heard her squeal. She hadn't been that loud.

"I know you're in there—I heard you."

The breath she'd been holding whooshed out of her on a well-fuck-me groan and she went and opened the door, regretting it immediately. Ian stood in the hallway wearing joggers, an Ice Knights hoodie, and a surly expression.

"It wasn't me," she said and started to shut the door before her pheromones got a whiff of him.

He stopped the door with his hand. "You saw it?" He pinched the bridge of his nose. "I was hoping to warn you before you saw it. Tell me you didn't read the comments. I swear to God, I'd like five minutes alone with some of those jackholes. It's bad enough that there was that lying article without having some dim-witted numbnuts call you a—" He stopped abruptly and grimaced. "Never mind. They're assholes."

Great. So not reading the comments had been her best decision ever. It had to be bad if Ian was all grumbly bear about it when he had barely spoken to her after one of her worst decisions ever to kiss him after that big goal.

"No comments. Got it." She looked pointedly at his hand on the door, already planning to sprint for her phone as soon as the door clicked shut because she was a total glutton for punishment. "Thanks."

He didn't let go of the door. Instead, he rubbed the back of his neck with his free hand, looking everywhere but at her as the tips of his ears got redder with each second. If she didn't know any better, she'd think he was embarrassed for coming to warn her. But that couldn't be right.

She pressed her palm against her stomach that was suddenly all sorts of jittery. "Do you want coffee?"

He nodded. "Sure."

Ian followed her inside, and all of a sudden her normal-size hotel room felt extra small. They were three tiny steps from the bed. Two normal steps to the couch. Four steps to the shower where they could get naked and—

"You gotta promise you won't read the comments," Ian said, interrupting her thoughts that had no business going the direction they were.

Doing her best to keep her hands steady, she put a pod in the coffee maker, poured in water, and hit start. "Are they that bad?"

His silence served as confirmation.

How completely awesome. This was just the way she wanted to start a new job. First, she accidentally spills a parentage secret, firebombing a friendship and sending the team into a losing spin cycle, and now she was the team skank. Did it get any better than this? God, she hoped so.

Straightening her shoulders, she lifted her chin and looked at a spot over Ian's left shoulder, determined to lie her ass off.

"Okay, well, as long as it wasn't anyone I care about saying it, I guess I'll live." She added a sassy chuckle as if absolutely none of this bothered her in the least. "I'll save reading the comments for when I have peanut butter cake nearby."

"Make jokes all you want, but thanks to my dad and my choice of careers, the media has made sure I know about other people's negative opinions of me for as long as I can remember," he said, looking her straight in the eyes, everything about him focused on her. "You don't want to let these people inside your head—it can be hard to get them out."

The way he said it without even a hint of sarcasm or teasing but with absolutely sincere concern hit her right in the chest and sent her pulse into the stratosphere. "Ian Petrov, are you looking out for me?"

He took a step closer so that they were nearly touching. "Yeah."

"Why?" The question was out before she thought about the fact that she may not want to hear the answer.

Really, who wanted to hear *because I pity you* or *we're part of the same team* or *because we're dinner buddies*? Not her—not when it came to someone she was having inappropriate thoughts about on a way-too-regular basis.

He gave her a look. It was the kind where his eyes went dark and intense and every fluttery part of her body—which she would have sworn hadn't existed—rose up in response. Maintaining eye contact was unimaginable. Glancing away was an impossibility.

"Because," he said, dipping his head lower, "I like you."

She laughed, that stupid high-pitched squeak of a giggle that always seemed to come out at the wrong time—like when the last guy she should be kissing looked at her like that. Luckily—or unluckily, she wasn't sure—he didn't pull back.

Instead, he cupped her face with his hands and kissed her, sending a sizzle of desire through her entire body. It wasn't hard. He teased her with his tongue, drawing her out until she couldn't help but kiss him back, closing the distance between their bodies and demanding more. All the reasons why this was a bad idea melted away under the heat of his touch. And just when she was ready to climb him like a tree because not being as close to him as possible wasn't an option, he broke the kiss and stepped back.

For as dazed and sexually frustrated as she felt at that

moment, it was nothing compared to the want in his eyes. Fucking A. Whatever happened next was going to go down in the history book of oh-my-God-yes, right next to standardizing bread being sold in sliced loaves and whoever thought of double espresso lattes.

But then, Ian just brushed his lips across her forehead and left without even one of his signature grunts. Meanwhile, she stood there, dumbstruck with her fingers pressed to her kiss-swollen lips, trying to untangled what in the world had just happened and what would happen next.

• • •

Attempting a breakaway while pulling a Zamboni would have been less difficult than leaving Shelby's hotel room. But he'd done it. Kissing her hadn't been part of his plan when he'd gone to her room.

Yeah, like you even had a plan, buddy.

All he'd known was that he didn't want her to have all those shitty comments in her head. The need to spare her that had gotten him out of his room before he'd even considered what he was doing. And then he'd kissed her, because not doing so was pretty much impossible and he didn't have a single fucking regret about it.

Not until he noticed that Christensen was standing in his open hotel room door, watching Ian as if he were the best reality TV show there was. He really should have checked the hallway first before walking out of Shelby's room. God knew what Christensen must be thinking.

Pretty much the same as you would be, boy-o.

Ian glared at the other man. "Why do you look so damn happy?"

"Because I was starting to lose patience waiting for you to make your move," Christensen said without any hint of embarrassment about getting caught gawking.

"What are you talking about?" He regretted the question as soon as it was out of his mouth.

This was what came from that practice session yesterday. Now the door had been cracked open between them, and keeping Christensen out would be that much harder. The guy knew him too well. That's why he'd had to shut everything down between them with brutal efficiency. The Ice Knights forward had the skill on and off the ice to find an opening.

"You walking out of Shelby's room with what looks like a smile on your face," Christensen said. "I mean, I can't be sure, since it's been so long since you've done anything but glower."

"Fuck off." Ian crossed over to his door.

"What, you're not interested in her?"

As if he was going to tell Christensen that. Instead, he just grunted and used his key card to unlock his door.

His former best friend made an exaggerated *huh* sound. "I'll take that as me being cleared to move in."

Ian knew what this was. It wasn't the first time Christensen had busted his chops like this—or he'd done it to him. Used to be it was their preferred pregame warm-up. Talk shit, let out the nerves, and get ready to go kick ass. If he thought he could use the same tactics to make him jealous, he had another think coming because he knew Shelby like Christensen never would.

"You really think she'd go for a never-shuts-up pretty boy like you?" he asked.

"Why not?" Christensen smirked. "Women find me irresistible."

Oh yeah. This guy was very much not Shelby's type. Who was her type? Ian was. "Okay, go for it. Knock on her door and try your best."

"I will."

"Go ahead."

Christensen looked at her closed door, the first twinge of oh-fuck-what-did-I-get-myself-into giving his face a pinched look. "Now?"

Ian crossed his arms and waited. One Mississippi. Two Mississippi. Three Mississippi.

Finally, the other man walked over to Shelby's door and gave it three quick taps.

Shelby opened it. "Hey, Alex. What's up?"

Christensen leaned against the doorjamb and gave her a grin that graced the billboard ads he got the big money for. "Just came by to say hi."

"Um, okay." She looked over at Ian, her eyebrows raised in question, and then back at Christensen. "Hi."

"So," Christensen said, "did you want to go grab coffee?"

"I've got some already brewed," she said. "But you're sweet to have thought of me."

He winked at her. "Anytime."

"Okay, then." She started to shut the door, first making eye contact with Ian as if to ask what was going on. "Bye."

As soon as the door shut, Ian did the slow clap. Okay, maybe he was the cocky asshole, but he had to go with his instinct. The Shelby who'd nearly laid him out with a Taser wasn't the type of woman to melt at Alex Christensen's insincere flirting.

Mind obviously blown, Christensen turned to him, his face scrunched up with confusion. "What the hell, man?"

Was he enjoying this moment a little too much? Probably, but he could live with that. "You don't understand a woman like Shelby."

Christensen scoffed. "And I suppose you do."

"Without a doubt." Now that was definitely a step too far, but he understood her a helluva lot better than his brother.

She had no time for bullshit. It was something they had

in common.

The elevator dinged its arrival at the end of the hall, and Coach Peppers walked out, carrying a steaming cup of coffee in a to-go cup. "There you are, Petrov." He took a sip and twisted his mouth in revulsion. No doubt because there was actually coffee in the cup as opposed to the 99 percent milk and sugar the coach was used to. "Doc's given you the all clear. You're playing tonight. I expect to be amazed by you two. Morning skate in an hour."

On. The. Ice. He was finally getting back. Jacked up on an instant shot of adrenaline, he turned to Christensen and held up his hand. His brother high-fived him before Ian even realized what he'd done. It's exactly what he would have done in the same situation before he'd found out they were brothers.

Christensen grinned at him. "Try to keep up tonight."

"Not gonna be a problem," he shot back and then went into his room to get ready for the morning skate.

Doing lazy loop-de-loops on the ice was one thing. Being in the mix of a morning skate was totally different. It was fucking magic. It always had been. Even when his dad had warned him that professional hockey wasn't for everyone when Ian got drafted late, he hadn't lost his love for it. The crisp air. The slice of his blades on the ice. The sound of the puck smacking on his stick. The high of watching the opposing goalie do a pretzel-bend trick and still not be able to stop the biscuit from crossing the line.

Three hours later, still riding that wave after a killer slap shot, he skated off the ice at the end of practice right toward the spot in the stands where Shelby sat typing away on her laptop. No doubt she was about to upload another update about the Ice Knights and the Petrov and Christensen show to The Biscuit's blog.

"Hey, Petrov," Alex called out from his spot by the bench.

"Coach says to go see him before showers."

Fuck. Really?

Without missing a stroke, he pivoted away from Shelby and toward the tunnel. But when he looked back over his shoulder, she was watching him skate away, her fingers pressed to her lips again, a slight blush making her cheeks pink, as if the rink had suddenly gotten twenty degrees warmer. Looking at her, he felt that heat wave himself.

"I'm sure it's just to go over the plan for tonight, since you've been out for so long," Christensen said, falling into step with him as they both got off the ice and walked on the rubber mats leading from the rink to the visitors' locker room.

"Pregame milks in the locker room?" Ian asked, pausing for a second before he had to turn right outside of the locker room to go to Coach's makeshift office.

Christensen's eyes widened with surprise. They hadn't chugged pregame milks in the locker room since the news that they shared a dad broke.

"I'll bring them," Christensen said, looking off past Ian as if there was something super interesting about the plain beige walls of the hallway.

Yeah. He got that. What did they have to say anyway? What was done was done.

Ramming his fingers through his sweaty hair, he turned and started toward Coach's office. A brother. How many times growing up had he wished for one? Too many to count. His sisters were great but a brother, that was just different. Now he had one. Maybe that wasn't the worst thing after all.

• • •

"What do you mean you've never been ice-skating?" Ian was trying to wrap his brain around that as he, Christensen, and Shelby had their usual team dinner at what everyone on the team was calling "the kiddie table."

It made no sense. To a man, every guy on the team had probably been in skates almost as soon as they could walk. Professional hockey players started young, and they never stopped if they wanted to make it to the NHL. Shelby—someone who lived and breathed hockey almost as much as he did—smoothed her fingers across the close-cropped side of her hair and shrugged.

She fidgeted with her napkin. "You say that as if everyone has been ice-skating. I really don't see what the big deal is."

Didn't.

See.

What.

The.

Big.

Deal.

Was?

The feel of fresh, smooth ice in a rink was all speed and adrenaline. A frozen pond? That was agility and quick reaction to the dips and divots in the top layer. Either way, skating was about as close to total freedom as he'd ever gotten, and that's what made the game so great. It wasn't just speed and skill, it was being strategic and knowing just when to lay a good hip check to take all that freedom away from an opposing player—and the puck, too.

Eyes practically popping out of his head, he glanced over at Christensen, who had the same big-eyed, what-the-fuck expression that Ian was sure he had on his own face. His brother looked over at him, and it was as if the past few months had never happened. In an instant, they had that old line of silent communication back again.

Raised eyebrow: *She has no clue what she's missing.*

Double raised eyebrows: *What do you think, go grab some unofficial ice time?*

Quick look around followed by a conspiratorial smile: *Really, it's the right thing to do.*

Clink of his glass to Christensen's: *You should do this.*

They both got up while Shelby looked from one of them to the other. "What's going on?"

"I'm taking you ice-skating," he said as he got up. "It'll be fun. I'll hold on to you and everything so you don't have to worry about falling."

As she stood up, a nervous giggle squeaked out and she slapped her palm over her mouth as if to hold in any more high-pitched noises. Her cheeks turned pink and she immediately looked over at the big table of Ice Knights players. It wasn't the first time she'd reacted like that whenever her volume went above the minimum. For someone who looked like such a badass, she seemed to just want to only be heard at the keyboard when she was writing for The Biscuit.

He couldn't explain the urge that had him reaching out to bring her hand down; he just went with it. "You have a great laugh."

She rolled her eyes at him, but it seemed to do the trick and the tension in her shoulders seeped out.

He and Shelby said their goodbyes to the rest of the team and walked out of the restaurant right into the blinding flash of the lone photographer lying in wait outside the door.

"So what's the story?" asked a guy with drips from today's lunch mixed in with the bright flowers of his Hawaiian shirt. "A little brotherly sharing?"

Ian had Shelby behind him and was in the other man's face in an instant. "Fuck you."

"Go ahead, big boy." The photographer took a few steps back as he lifted his camera and grabbed a few quick shots. "I'll get the whole thing in pics and sue you for all you've got."

"You're an asshole," Ian snarled, an angry fire eating its way up from his gut.

"That may be," the other man said as he walked away. "But at least I don't have to fight for the scraps left by my dad and brother."

And that's when all of Ian's locks clicked into place, one after the other, dead bolts turning closed so that the anger was shut away behind layers of steel and titanium. His breaths became longer, slower, his gaze cleared as all the red fury dissipated, and everything inside him went icy cold. It was exactly what had happened when he'd heard that he and Christensen shared half their DNA, exactly what had happened the first time in college when a national sports reporter said he was a cheap copy of the old man, and exactly what happened every time his dad stood on the other side of the wall at the rink and watched Ian's practices with barely concealed disappointment.

Shelby stepped closer, slipping her fingers between his and squeezing. "We can just head back to the hotel."

"No, that asshole isn't going to stop us." He'd learned that early. People would talk, they'd try to cut him open and take a peek inside, but he'd never really let them see. He refused to open up in front of them. It's how he stayed safe. He wasn't about to forget that lesson and let the gawkers win now. "Come on—it'll be fun."

...

Shelby and Ian obviously had different definitions of fun. His was balancing on teeny-tiny blades without letting his ankles wobble while going backward. Hers was eating store-bought raw cookie dough from a bucket.

"You've got this," Ian said, his hands holding hers in a strong, steady grip as he guided her around the practice facility's ice. "Just keep it steady."

That was easy for him to say—he didn't feel like a newborn

calf out here all jelly legs and lurching from foot to foot.

"You're doing great," Ian said, clearly in his element. He hadn't teetered once.

Keeping her eyes on her borrowed skates—who knew the team trainer and she had the same size feet?—she did a shuffle sorta glide thing to move forward. "You're a horrible liar."

"I don't do it often."

"I know. That's what I like about you."

They took one more half turn around the ice before he led her back over to the wall so she could clutch the top of the divider between the rink and the bench. Meanwhile, he went over it like he was hopping a fence. Show-off.

Yeah, one you can't take your eyes off now that you aren't afraid of face-planting.

She could look. It was touching that was the problem. She was totally in control about that. Nothing to worry about. Nope. Which was why she was ignoring the "danger, danger" siren blaring in her head and her breath caught when he lifted his arms to stretch and the hem of his shirt went up, showing off the bottom half of a six pack she desperately wanted to lick.

That is very much not a good idea, Shelby, no matter how tempting.

And it was so very, very tempting.

"So your parents never took you to a rink?" Ian asked as he unscrewed the thermos he'd brought from the visitors' locker room along with the skates.

"My mom was usually working a couple of jobs and hunting for her next husband in her off time." The drama, the excitement, the loosey-goosey thrill of first falling for someone, that's the part that had always been addictive for her mom. "There has never been a person who loved love like my mom. It was her hobby."

"Not yours?" He handed her the thermos.

The smell of hot chocolate wafted up from the opening, and she took a small sip before answering. "No, I went in for peach schnapps and then cheap gin."

"Started early?"

Did freshman year of high school count as early? Probably. "Quit early, too."

"What happened?"

Usually people danced around the subject. Not Ian. He went at it head-on, just like a face-off in the circle. It might annoy some people, but she appreciated the honesty of it. Somehow it made whatever was sizzling between them feel more solid, possible. That way was dangerous thinking, but she couldn't seem to help it around him.

"I went to rehab after hitting rock bottom." More like landing with a hard splat against it. "I'd lied to myself about not having a problem. I woke up one morning in the drunk tank, no money, no apartment anymore, and no friends who weren't sick of my self-destructive behavior. I went back home. I thought that would fix everything." Naive? Hopeful? Delusional? Probably a mix of all three. "Can you believe it didn't? It went badly. My mom got a counselor and staged an intervention. It sure wasn't pretty, but we got through it. I went to rehab. Then I went again a few months later—relapses are no joke. And now here I am, six years later flirting with disaster again."

"My name's Ian, not disaster."

Oh God. The man was bad at jokes. Still, she was chuckling even as she attempted to glide back from the wall while maintaining her balance. "I'm talking about this job. It changed everything for me, gave The Biscuit some legitimacy. Do you know how hard that can be for a woman-led hockey blog?"

She wobbled left and then right and threw her arms

outward to grab hold of the wall, but she missed it. Instead she clamped on to a strong forearm right as she tipped backward. The motion pulled him forward and he let out a loud "oof" as he hit the half wall in front of the bench. Fast as a heartbeat, he grabbed her flailing free hand and pulled her to the wall so she could grasp it and get her balance back.

"Oh my God." Heart beating so fast her pulse sounded like a tsunami in her ears, she looked up at him as he grimaced. "Did I break you?"

One side of his mouth shot up in a smirk. "You should definitely check me out."

"Why? What hurts, I—" Realization hit. He was fucking with her. "I don't get it. You're grunting one minute and joking the next."

He shrugged and came back out on the ice with her. "Like you said, I'm an onion."

"Okay, Shrek."

It seemed like the most natural thing in the world to take his hand—for balance support, of course—as they slow skated around the rink.

"You don't think I'm a man of great depth?"

He did a spin move so he was again going backward and they were face-to-face, holding hands, alone together in the practice facility. Her mom would call it romantic. She knew better. This was trouble in man form.

"What happened back there with the photographer?"

He pulled his arms in, tugging her closer but still leaving space so their skates didn't tangle. "He was a jackass."

She wasn't in disagreement there. "Yeah, but I'm talking about when you went into robot mode. You just shut down completely."

"So what? You as a member of the media are trying to get me to spill my trade secrets for surviving the media?"

"Is that how you think of me?" Ow. That landed with a

big thump right against her solar plexus. "That I'm like the paparazzi guy?"

"Of course not." Ian did a half turn so they were hip to hip, holding hands as they skated.

She glanced over at him, having instant lusty ideas about the feel of his beard scruff against her skin before yanking herself back to reality. "Then 'fess up."

"For as long as I can remember, there has been media." His jaw hardened and he looked up into the stands as if he expected a reporter or photographer to be up there now documenting his every move. "First it was all about my dad; then they started to actually look at me. They weren't really doing that, though." He smiled. It wasn't a nice one, more of a defense mechanism than a sign of happiness. "They were looking to see how I measured up against the old man. The judgment was always the same: a poor man's David Petrov."

Those fuckers. She wanted to find them now and she'd... well, she didn't know what but something. "That's not fair. You're—"

"A journeyman player," he interrupted. "I get that. I've made peace with it. I love the game, but I'm not going to be a Hall of Famer like my dad or a career that lasts decades like Christensen—the real recipient of the Petrov hockey talent."

He said it as if it didn't matter, but she wasn't fooled. No one got to this level of play unless they wanted to be the best. Ian may not be good at lying to her, but he seemed to excel at lying to himself.

"I've got another year or two, and then I'll go into coaching. I'm actually looking forward to it." This time his grin was genuine, but it faded quickly. "Of course, that's not the story the media will report. For them it will be all about my failures."

"Change the narrative." The ideas popped into her head one after the other. "You could—"

He lifted their hands, brushing his lips across her knuckles in a move that sent a sizzle of desire zinging through her.

"It's not worth it." He lowered their hands again. "There is nothing in the world worth opening myself up to everyone's judgment and splashing myself all over the hockey sites."

"Is that why you grunt so much?" she asked, lightening the mood with a teasing question.

"Maybe it's because I don't know what to say around you."

She snorted in disbelief. "Like the girl with the voice of a ten-year-old is in the least bit intimidating."

"I'm not intimidated," he said, bringing them to a stop right at center ice and turning all of his attention to her. "I'm fascinated."

Oh my.

Oh.

My.

His gaze dropped to her mouth as tactile as a touch that set her on fire and all she wanted was to get licked by the flames.

"We'd better get back to the hotel before curfew," she said, fumbling to hold on to her better judgment. "Can't break the rules."

"Not that one anyway."

Not any of them, because when it came to Ian Petrov, she wasn't sure she'd be able to go back again to pretending there was nothing between them.

Chapter Thirteen

This was a dumb decision.

Still, here Ian was, the night before the last game of the road trip, standing outside Shelby's Vancouver hotel room at one in the morning with a brand-new black eye and absolutely no idea what he was going to do. He should turn around and go right back to his room. He'd spent Seattle and Vegas trying to keep his distance as much as he could when they spent every meal and more together. But tonight, he'd been lying on his bed staring at the ceiling

Oh, fuck it.

He tapped lightly on her door. If she was sleeping, she wouldn't hear and he'd go back to his room. She was probably asleep anyway and— The door opened.

Wearing a black tank top that dipped low over the upper swells of her tits and leggings that made her legs seem even longer, Shelby stood in the opening. All the racket thundering in his head since the game ended, spurred on by adrenaline and an overtime win, settled.

The TV was on behind her but there wasn't any sound.

The covers on her bed were rumpled, but the pillows were propped up on the headboard as if she'd been sitting up in bed, not lying down trying to sleep.

"Is everything okay?" She stepped close, looking up at him with concern, her attention focusing in on his latest injury. "Do you need help? Is it your eye? That was such a cheap shot from Evanston. Total high stick."

"I'm fine." He managed to stifle the urge to touch the heart of the bruise where Doc had given him two quick stitches before sending him back out for the second period. "I couldn't sleep."

She crossed her arms and narrowed her gaze, the little vee of worry wrinkling her forehead smoothing out into are-you-kidding-me annoyance. "I am not currently accepting booty calls."

Way to go, Petrov. So smooth. Amazing. How are women not falling at your feet wherever you go?

"It's not that."

She lifted an eyebrow. "Uh-huh. If I invite you in, the next step in the plan is to tell me that you just want to stretch out and we'd both be more comfortable on the bed?"

"Is that the kind of guy you think I am?" He wasn't. He was a grown-ass man, not a frat boy.

She looked down at her bare wrist as if she were wearing a watch. "It's after midnight and you just knocked on my hotel door to tell me you couldn't sleep."

Okay, she had a point. And if he understood why in the hell he was there instead of watching episodes of *The Office* that he'd seen a million times already, per usual for a road trip, he would have told her. Instead, the best he could do was try not to sound as lame as he felt at the moment.

He shoved his hands in the pockets of his hoodie. "These will stay here the whole time."

She sighed and shook her head, but instead of closing the

door in his face, she opened it up farther and stepped back. "Don't make me regret this."

"Never."

At least not on purpose.

...

Shelby had just hit post on her latest dispatch for The Biscuit, so everything was scattered in her room—yeah, that was definitely her bra in the middle of the bed—and her head was equally a mess, which was the only sorta reasonable explanation she could give for letting Ian into her hotel room at one in the morning.

There was no way this was a good idea, but there was no way she was turning him away.

The truth was that she didn't want to.

It was their last night on the road. Tomorrow after the game, they'd be back on the team plane and headed to reality and Harbor City. No more late-night ice-skating lessons or dinners together or riding up in hotel elevators so close that they could touch but keeping their distance because once they did, she wasn't sure she'd be able to stop.

Hands stuffed in his pockets, Ian glanced over at her silent TV with the captions turned on. "*The Office?*"

"Comfort watch." She needed something in the background to distract her or else she would have been thinking about him instead of finishing her last post from the road.

He nodded, then his attention was centered back on her—hot and intense. "It's what I had on, too."

"So tomorrow night after the game, we fly home," she said, floundering for something to talk about when chitchat was the last thing she wanted with Ian in her room.

"No more dinners at the kiddie table."

She shook her head. "Nope."

Wow. Amazing repartee, Shelby.

Really, it was the best she could do under the circumstances. Ian Petrov was here in her hotel room and all she wanted was to finish what he'd started with that kiss.

Because I like you.

Who said that and then walked away? Ian Petrov, the hottest and most frustrating man she knew.

They stood next to each other, barely a few steps apart. His hands were still stuffed in his hoodie pockets, but that didn't make a difference. Every nerve in her body was tuned in to him. The urge to be closer to him had her taking another step toward him before she realized what she was doing. His hands were still in his pockets. Hers should be, too.

Instead, her fingertips burned with the need to touch him—to trace the line of his jaw, glide over the hard planes of his chest, to stroke and feel and memorize him. It was all she could do to ignore that need building inside her, making her whole body melt when all he was doing was looking at her.

"We can't," she said, sounding as if it wasn't a statement but a breathy question even to her own ears.

He stood still as a statue while the air between them was heavy with anticipation. "I know."

"I want to." Like a scuba diver needed an oxygen tank. Her lungs were tight as desire whipped through her, a wildfire on the verge of getting out of control.

He nearly closed the distance between them, still not touching her but coming oh so close, and gave her a half grin. "My hands have to stay in my pockets."

That was all it took to break her. The smart-ass response accompanied by the small lift of one side of his lips into that crooked smile of his—cocky and teasing all at once. It gave a glimpse of the man beneath the grunts and the growly attitude he tried to project as his true self. But she knew better. It was a cover, just like going cold around the media. The real Ian

Petrov had layers.

"Are you saying you're only good with your hands?" she asked.

He dipped his head lower until his lips nearly brushed the shell of her ear. "You know that isn't true."

Desire, hot and needy, made her breath catch. "Why don't you remind me?"

He took a step back. It was only a few inches but it felt like miles.

"You sure about this?" he asked, his body tense and hard, the outline of his thickening cock visible against the soft bottom of his joggers. "I can leave right now."

One last night. One final time. That's all this would be. It's all it could be. She'd pretend that was enough.

"We're not in Harbor City." She closed the distance between them. "Everyone knows that being outside of your own zip code doesn't count."

And she kissed him.

• • •

Ian took his hands out of his pockets.

There was no way he could leave without touching Shelby. The cotton of her tank top was a thin barrier between them, but it was still too much. He needed more. He needed her.

As if reading his mind—or as desperate as he was—she broke the kiss to take off her tank. After that, it was like they'd flipped a switch. Clothes went flying as they raced to get rid of it all, the need to touch bare skin, to kiss and lick and nip every inch overwhelming anything else.

Deepening the kiss, he skimmed his hands down her sides, gliding over the swell of her hips before cupping her ass and lifting her up. She wrapped her legs around him. Her fingers in his hair, pulling and demanding more. He trailed his lips down her neck, pulling her closer against him so he could better fit his cock against her.

"God, you feel so good." He squeezed her ass, watching as she bit down on her lip, the move drawing his attention to that lush mouth of hers.

"I want to feel you," she said, her voice husky with want. "But you need to put me down."

He hated to let her go, but telling her no was an impossibility. "Touch away," he said after he lowered her feet to the floor but let his fingers linger on her hips.

Then she did the last thing he expected: She let go. "Hands on the wall."

He had a half second of hesitation before he did exactly as she wanted.

Palms pressed against the wall, he let out a tortured groan the second she wrapped her long fingers around his cock and started to stroke.

She paused. "Too tight?"

"Too good."

She smiled up at him. "Let's see if there's room for improvement anyway."

She slid her hand down to the base of his cock and sucked the head into her mouth. Jesus. It was soft and hard, wet and dry, slick and steady all in one instant. It was more pleasure than his brain could process, but there was no way in the world he was going to tell her to stop or slow down or anything at all—not in any small part because forming words was beyond his abilities right now. Up and down, in and out, over and over until his dick was so hard and wet and ready for more that he was grounding his molars together to keep from coming.

She wasn't done with him, though. Her free hand cupped his balls, squeezing and rolling them with just enough power to take it even higher. Then she stroked a finger over the sensitive spot behind his balls at the same time that she took him in her mouth all the way to the back of her throat. He clenched his eyes shut and used every ounce of willpower he had to stay on the edge instead of spilling over. Hands curled into fists of desperation, he kept his knuckles pressed to the wall and teetered as she did something with her tongue that he didn't have the vocabulary to describe but fucking A, did it feel good.

Too good, unless he wanted his part in this to be over too soon.

"Shelby," he said, barely getting her name out.

She stopped and looked up, her eyes wide and her lips wet from sucking him. "You want something else?"

"I want it all." He'd never said something truer in his life.

He reached down and pulled her up so she was standing, her legs spread wide and her back against the wall. Damn, she was beautiful. Unable to not give in to temptation, he took a step back and looked his fill, gripping his dick hard at the base to alleviate some of the pressure.

She smoothed her hands over her curves. "You like what you see?"

"I love what I'm about to taste."

He went to his knees in front of her and buried his face in her sweet pussy. She was slick and ready for him. Hands on the inside of her strong thighs, he explored her with his tongue, tasting her desire, and she moaned and rocked against his face. Oh yeah, his Shelby wanted what he could give her.

Looking up at her as he leaned back on his heels and circled her clit with his thumb, he savored having her on his lips. "So very good, aren't you?"

"Ian," she said, her voice getting breathy. "Don't play with me."

"You don't want me to go slow and take my time?" Was he being an ass? Absolutely.

"No."

"What do you want, Shelby?"

She let out a desperate moan. "You know."

"Say it." It wasn't that he didn't want to take the time to explore her. God, did he. However, there was something about seeing her demand what she wanted, pull in control, and take it that he was desperate to see.

"I want to come." She rotated her hips as if she couldn't help but move like she wanted to be touched. "I need it."

"Are you gonna ride my face?"

She got a look in her eyes—bright and intense—as she exhaled a shaky breath. "Yes."

"Are you going to use my mouth to get off?" He took her hand, moving it over his lips, sucking on her fingertips as he did.

"Yes."

"Then do it." And he leaned forward, tongue pressing to her clit and his fingers slowly circling her entrance.

She didn't take it easy on him, and he loved it. Fingers in his hair, she steered him where she wanted him, urging him to go harder, faster, slower, softer as she rocked against his mouth until she let out a cry and came on his lips.

• • •

With her back against the wall and her thighs shaking, Shelby tried to catch her breath. Good God. How in the hell was she still upright?

Ian stood up in front of her and leaned in, kissing her with a possessive intensity that had her body aching for him. The bed was too damn far. That chair over there, though. That was an option.

Without hesitating, she dipped underneath his arms and walked to the club chair. Giving him a sassy look, she winked and then bent over the back of the chair, keeping her legs spread.

"Fuck," Ian said, the single word sounding more like a prayer than a curse. "I could look at you spread out like this for me all night."

She looked back and gave him a mock glare. "Don't you dare."

"You're done waiting, huh?" he asked, obviously teasing her as he rolled on a condom while crossing to her. "I know the feeling." He slid the tip of his dick over her slick core. "Damn, baby. I love the sight of this. The feel of you. Everything. I love it all."

It wa just the high of the moment, she knew that, but still it would be easy to believe he meant more because the truth was she wanted it to.

He liked her.

She was falling for him.

Before the potential impact of that important distinction could hit, though, Ian sank into her, pushing away everything except for how he made her feel. Hands on her hips, he squeezed just enough to anchor her to him as he slid in and out of her, going a little bit deeper each time until she was filled with him. Already primed by her first orgasm, her body responded to the rhythm they set together. After each stroke forward, he pulled her back against him as he pistoned in and out of her, hard, demanding, just what she needed. This wasn't about making love. It wasn't about release. This was desperation and need and knowing that no matter how much she got, it wouldn't be enough. She wasn't sure it ever could be. When it came to Ian Petrov, she didn't want now—she wanted forever.

"Fuck, baby. So damn good." He reached a hand around the front of her waist and slipped two fingers between her legs. "I want to feel you come around my dick."

With the way he was circling her clit, that wasn't going to be a problem.

"That's it. Rock against me. Show me what you want."

She arched her back, changing the angle enough so that his cock rubbed against her entrance at just the right spot. Her thighs quivered as she tensed, her climax tightening into a ball of energy until it exploded, her orgasm slamming into her.

Ian's grip tightened as she rode the wave of pleasure and he pumped into her once, twice more before burying himself as deep as he could and coming hard.

As they sank to the floor, sated, exhausted, both still floating a bit, Shelby blocked out that little voice that was already starting to whisper evil nothings in her ear. It was just the one last time. It may have meant more to her than to him, but that was okay. It wasn't like a relationship between the two of them could work out. They'd both worked too hard to get to where they wanted to be in the hockey world to lose it all now.

"Stop thinking so loud." He dropped the used condom in the nearby trash can and then scooped her up and carried her to the bed. "Nap first. Round two second."

She loved the sound of that, but it probably wasn't the best plan of action. "Who said you could stay the night?"

He sat down on the bed with her, pulling the covers up over her. "Do you want me to go?"

Ignoring the warning siren blaring in her head, she told the truth. "No."

He smiled and tucked an arm around her waist, pulling her in snugly against him. "Good."

Unlike at the cabin, Ian was out in minutes while she stared at the ceiling for an hour wondering what was going to happen next before finally drifting off without any answers about what was going to happen next.

Chapter Fourteen

Shelby was in a world of shit. She was smelling a hotel pillow. Also, she was wearing the hoodie Ian had left behind when he'd hurried out of her room shortly after dawn. Okay, shortly after round three and right before the team's morning skate.

After finally setting the pillow aside, she reached for a leftover room service chocolate croissant and scrolled through the morning hockey headlines on her phone. Maybe there was some sort of *My Strange Addiction* episode she should apply to be on—pillow sniffers anonymous. That had to rank right up there with the one about the people who ate their own couch cushions.

A text notification popped up on her screen accompanied by a picture of a sparkling emerald green Mustang Shelby GT350 with a crisp white racing stripe down the middle of the hood.

Roger: *How's my favorite mustang?*

Shelby: *Purring like I've just pulled onto the straightaway.*

Damn, it was the truth. Who knew orgasms and midnight room service could do that for a woman?

Roger: *That's what I like to hear. Any trouble finding those meetings on the road?*

Shelby: *Smooth sailing.*

She'd gone to a church basement meeting in Denver and another in Vegas. Both had the same bad coffee and stomach-settling coming-home feeling. Even after six years, that sense never went away. Meetings may not always be a comfortable place, but they were always a safe place.

Roger: *And the rest of things? Job?*

Shelby: *Job's good. The rest? My head's above water.*

She wasn't about to explain the mess that was whatever it was with her and Ian to her sponsor. She loved Roger, but she really needed to get better girlfriends. Talking about sexy times with him really just felt all sorts of wrong.

Roger: *Do you need to hop on the phone?*

Shelby: *I'm good, thanks, Dad.*

Roger: *I'd be a lucky guy if that were the case.*

Shelby: *You're a softie.*

Not that anyone would guess it from looking at him. Wiry. Flinty. More likely to yell at someone to get off his lawn than buy Girl Scout cookies? Yeah, that was her sponsor. But underneath it all? Total teddy bear. Sorta like someone else she knew.

Roger: *You back tonight?*

Shelby: *Yep.*

Roger: *Let's meet up for diner milkshakes later on in the week.*

Shelby: *So you can make faces when I dip my fries into my chocolate shake?*

Roger: *It's our tradition. Text when you get back to the city.*

After sending a goodbye text, she did not take one more sniff of the pillow that smelled like Ian—okay, an extra-deep inhale, but that didn't count—and got in the shower. Then she headed out of her room for the rink and the afternoon face-off. It wasn't until her alerts dinged on her cell phone that she checked the latest hockey news again. When she did, her belly dropped faster than an elevator with its ropes cut.

Daddy Petrov In Vancouver to Watch His Boys?

There wasn't much of a story to go with the headline beyond a short clip of David Petrov standing outside the Vancouver arena signing autographs and giving the reporter a curt "no comment" when asked about his sons. Her gut sank anyway. David the Great was in Vancouver. This was not going to end well. Not even a little.

• • •

It was the first question a reporter asked Ian about in the post-game interviews. Not about Stuckey's massive hit on Eggleton. Not about Christensen's breakaway goal. Not about Blackburn's call to arms in the locker room before they came out in the third period and came back from a three-to-one deficit to win in a shootout. No. The first thing everyone wanted to know about was what the great David Petrov had said about the game.

Ian exhaled a deep breath and the locks went down one by one. *Click. Click. Click.* "I haven't talked to him."

"Your dad rarely comes to games. Do you know why he is here tonight?" One of the reporters shoved an iPhone in Ian's face. "Have you guys cleared the air? Seems like you and your brother have mended fences."

"I'll talk about the game." Ian looked around at the locker room. Players were mostly dressed, packing up their stuff, and the vibe was good. Winning did that for a team. "Any questions there?"

"Oh, come on," another reporter called out. "You gotta give us something."

He could practically hear the metal whine as those mental locks were tested. The cool was his thing. He'd always done it. Cold. Unemotional. Robotic. But a man could only take that for so long. Eventually, the screws holding the locks in place would get stripped and break free. Then all hell was going to break lose.

That couldn't happen, but the urge was there, dark and growing.

But before it could explode, Christensen appeared by his side out of nowhere, dressed but still dripping from the shower. He slung his arm around Ian's shoulders as the cameras zoomed in on the first public showing of brotherly love.

"He gave you one helluva game," Christensen said, his tone friendly and open. "If it hadn't been for his perfect pass, I wouldn't have been able to make it down the ice for that breakaway."

One of the TV reporters asked, "Have you talked to your dad?"

Ian tensed, unease swirling in his gut like radioactive battery acid.

Christensen snorted. "Not since I took some very bad advice from him." He jerked his chin over to where Lucy stood shooting electric dirty looks toward the scrum of reporters surrounding them. "Now, it looks like Lucy is calling you guys over. Trust me, she is not a woman you ever want to ignore."

The reporters let out a collective groan and turned like a group of fourth graders headed to the principal's office.

The farther they moved away, the more the muscles in his shoulder loosened. "Thanks, man," he said to Christensen.

His brother grinned. "Let's go get on the bus before we're stuck with the shitty seats."

They walked out of the locker room and down the hall leading to the parking garage. They made it a third of the way through before a familiar voice stopped him in his tracks.

"My boys together," David Petrov said, looking at the two of them as if they'd welcome him with open arms. "This is quite the sight."

"Why are you here?" Ian asked, not bothering to pretend to make it sound pleasant.

Dave gave them an easy grin. It was like seeing Christensen's smile out of an older version of Ian's own face. "Fucking creepy" didn't even begin to cover it. Nor how he never noticed it before.

"I wanted to talk," he said.

Of course.

Ian cut a glance at Christensen, who rolled his eyes. At least they were on the same play. This wasn't about anything other than what David Petrov wanted at the moment. How fucking typical.

Christensen crossed his arms. "So say what you need to say."

"How about if we go grab some food or something? I can get you to the airport instead of you having to take the team bus." He took a few steps away, as if they were going to follow him. "I was always starving after a game."

Neither Ian nor Christensen moved.

"I'm fine," Ian said.

His brother nodded. "Me too."

David's steps stilled and he turned, the dear-old-dad easiness gone from his stance, and he pointed at the two of them. "Look, I know you're upset, but we're a team. You two have to move past what happened before."

Ian and Christensen looked at each other.

Christensen raised an eyebrow: *The fuck?*

Ian tilted his head to the left: *Fuck if I know.*

Christensen rolled his eyes: *What a dick.*

Ian snorted: *Agreed.*

Conversation complete, Ian dead-eye stared at their dad. "How are we a team?"

"You're my boys."

As if that made a difference.

"So you donated DNA," Christensen said. "What's the point?"

The man everyone thought they knew, the beloved scoring machine disappeared completely. "I was there for you from the beginning," he said, his top lip curling. "I provided for both of you. Neither of you wanted for anything." He tossed up his hands in frustration. "And what do I get in return? Both of you acting like petulant children. That reflects badly on me."

"And there it is. The real reason you're here." Ian laughed. Loud. Hard. Without a single ounce of joy. "So your legacy's taking a hit, huh?"

David stiffened. "My records still stand."

"For now," Christensen said with all the cockiness a future Hall of Famer could deliver. "Is there anything else?"

"Just cut the poor-me-my-feelings-are-hurt shit and

toughen up, boys."

Christensen looked at Ian and shook his head. "Damn, can you believe I used to dream about getting life advice from my dad?"

"Really?" God, Ian had spent his life trying to get the advice to stop. "He's total shit at it."

Their dad let out an angry huff. "You two take after your mothers."

He and Christensen looked at each other, relieved grins on their faces. "Thank fucking God," they said at the same time.

And that's when he spotted Shelby walking straight toward them, a hesitant slowness to her step as if she wasn't sure if she'd be welcome. He was halfway to her before he thought about it and realized what that would mean. By the time he reached her, it was too late.

His dad transformed as soon as he spotted her. Gone was the snarl and the palpable disgust, replaced with that easygoing charm that had always been David Petrov's costume.

"Hi there." He stuck out his hand. "David Petrov."

The fake-humble attitude had always been his dad's go-to—but Shelby didn't know any better. For her, he'd always be the great David Petrov, king of the ice and holder of multiple scoring records.

"I know who you are, sir." She shook his hand. "I'm Shelby Blanton."

"With The Biscuit?" His dad's eyes lit up with what would look like sincerity to someone who didn't know him better. "Wow. That site is great. Huge fan."

She nearly melted into a puddle right there. "That means a lot."

"Well, I know you guys have a flight to catch. Good to see you again." He turned to Shelby. "Wonderful to finally put a gorgeous face with a kickass site. Keep up the good work."

Then he walked away down the tunnel—in the direction of the reporters, of course. No doubt, he'd pull his usual no-comment routine that always seemed to drive up interest.

"So you guys are talking again?" she asked, practically beaming with hope. "Oh, thank God. I was so worried. He seems like he's really making an effort to fix things."

"Yeah," Ian said, grinding out the word through clenched teeth. "He's quite a guy."

Years of training, of knowing that to tell the truth about his dad would only mean more scrutiny from the press, more second-guessing of his every move, and more ridiculous think pieces purporting to be a deep dive into his private life, kept him from saying more.

All he was, sometimes all it seemed he would ever be, was a reflection of his dad. It was easier to keep it on lockdown, to let the world believe the lie—especially when it came to Shelby, because letting her see that part of his life, that would be admitting too much about him and about how he felt about her.

• • •

A half hour into the flight back home and Shelby had run out of small talk. It didn't help that Ian had gone back into cabin grunt mode. Sitting next to him, she searched for anything to maybe draw the moment out a little more. As soon as they were wheels down in Harbor City, everything changed. No more dinners. No more ice-skating. No more devouring a midnight bowl of room service ice cream while sitting naked in the bed.

She wasn't ready for that yet.

The anticipation of landing had her fiddling with her six-year chip, rubbing the pad of her thumb over the plastic ridges to ground herself to the here and now. In a moment of desperation, she grabbed hold of the first thing she could think of that they hadn't talked about so far. "So that's pretty cool about your dad coming to see you guys."

The muscle in Ian's jaw twitched as he continued to look out the team jet's window.

"Maybe we could have a dinner with the three of you." The words rushed out. Another dinner would mean more time with Ian. An excuse to see him, spend time with him. Pathetic? Yeah, but desperate times and all. "I could include it in the final post for the series about you and Alex."

He let out a short huff of breath. "Not even if it meant getting traded to the Rage."

"What is going on, Ian?" Everything had seemed fine this morning. Beyond fine, really. Now? It was like he'd gone back behind that wall he used to shut people out. "Talk to me."

"Why?" He pivoted in his seat, keeping his voice low. "For the clicks?"

She flinched. "That's a low blow."

He opened his mouth, closed it, and then waited a few beats while clenching his jaw closed so fiercely, she worried the team dentist was going to have a new client.

"Nothing with my dad," he said. "That's nonnegotiable."

"I understand." She reached out and gave his leg a quick squeeze, then drew back before anyone saw. "You're still getting used to everything."

It was hard for a person to find out that their family wasn't exactly what they thought it was. She still remembered the drop in her stomach when she'd found out that the man she'd thought would never leave had. After that, everything had changed.

"Not every story has a happy ending, Shelby," Ian said, his tone resigned. "Some things are best left alone."

Her stomach sank. Was he just talking about his dad now,

or was he trying to tell Shelby something more?

Ian fell asleep—or more likely pretended to—and she stared at the movie playing on her iPad screen while not taking in a single moment of the plot. So this was just what they'd said. A fling. As long as they weren't in one of the Harbor City zip codes, the clothes could come off. The emotions, though, stayed covered. That was the deal. But fuck if she wasn't starting to feel naked as hell right about now.

Shelby, what have you done?

Chapter Fifteen

The taste of salty fries and a chocolate shake still fresh the next day, Shelby walked the block and a half from the diner she and Roger had met at to catch up to the Ice Knights arena with an extra spring in her step. As she got closer to the staff entrance, a man in head-to-toe Cajun Rage gear stubbed out a cigarette and walked toward her.

"I thought you gave those up, Bill," she said, giving the Cajun Rage's vice president of communications a quick hug.

"It was just so I had an excuse to hang outside in hopes of running into you."

When she'd been starting The Biscuit, almost all the teams ignored her requests for interviews. Not Bill. He'd treated her like one of hockey's own. It had been refreshing. A Bill who was also a friend of Bill W's, they'd met at an AA meeting shortly after she'd gotten out of rehab. One evening later over coffee, deep dish pie, and "oohing" and "ahhhing" over the pictures of him and his husband on their wedding anniversary trip to Antarctica, they'd become friends.

"Congrats on the deal with the Ice Mites," he said, using

the Rage fan's favorite nasty nickname for the Ice Knights. "Wish we would have thought of snagging you first."

"Like I'd ever go work for the Cajun Lame?" She shook her head. "Forget about it."

"I figured, but the door's always open. We're huge fans of The Biscuit," he said, glancing at his watch. "Don't be such a stranger, kid. We're due for a dinner."

"You got it." Since her social calendar was pretty much as blank as it ever was, that wasn't going to be a problem. "And thanks for the job offer. I'll keep it in mind."

"Well, at least let me buy you a frozen lemonade after tonight's game. We can talk about how much better the restaurants are in New Orleans than Harbor City."

As if that was even possibly true. "You're gonna have to buy me two pink lemonades to make up for such lies."

"Deal," he said with a chuckle and held open the door for her.

They walked in together but split up at the end of the hallway. He went toward the end with the visitors' locker room and she went toward the Ice Knights' side. Maybe she slowed down a little outside the locker room and slow rolled it in hopes of seeing Ian. Okay, she totally did that. There was just no denying the flutter of butterflies in her stomach whenever she thought of him or the spark of desire or the curiosity about what he was thinking or the…well, everything.

As if the universe was smiling down on her, the locker room door opened and Ian walked out. He wasn't in uniform yet, but he had on his game face—an unshaven square jaw tense with determination, a sense of barely controlled power and aggression. It shouldn't turn her on, but it did.

"Hey there," she said, trying to sound somewhat normal and not like she was about to go up in flames.

He didn't say anything, at least not with words. The intensity in his stare, though, said a lot.

"Shelby, is that you?" asked a man from behind her, whose voice was so familiar despite not having talked to him for years.

She turned and there he was. Jasper Dawson stood with Lucy near the VIP entrance to the arena. No more than five eight, he always managed to seem bigger than he was, even when he was standing next to the very tall Lucy.

"I cannot believe it is Shelby Blanton right in front of my eyes." He came over, his walk as fast as ever. "How are you and why didn't you tell anyone that I'm your stepdad? Lucy just told me she had no idea about our connection."

Emotion clogging her throat, she blinked away the wetness gathering in her eyes. This man was going to make her cry. She had no idea that he'd remember her and yet, here he was calling himself her dad. "Well, you'll always be my favorite stepdad, but I wanted to earn a spot here on my own, of course."

"You sure did that," he said, grinning at her as if he really was her proud papa. "Give me a hug."

She had absolutely no intention of saying no. The hug was solid, comforting, and just what she didn't realize she needed.

"You know," he said after the hug. "The hardest part of divorcing your mother was not getting to hang out with you anymore."

"Yeah, we moved to Florida as soon as the papers were signed." Not an exaggeration. She and her mom had driven a U-Haul to the lawyer's office and had left straight after.

"I'm glad to have you back here like old times." He turned to Lucy and Ian. "We used to watch the games right behind the bench, and she'd always manage to beat me when it came to Ice Knights trivia and I'd have to buy her one of those deep-fried-Oreo monstrosities."

"I can't believe you remember that."

"We were friends," he said. "I hope we can be again.

Your mom's doing okay, I hope."

Oh Lord. Whatever it was with her mom and the men she married, she never left a single one mad. They all came back around. "Yeah, she's in the 'burbs just north of Harbor City."

Jasper got a faraway look in his eye that left him with a big smile on his face. "I'll have to look her up."

"Watch out—she's still herself," Shelby warned.

"That's what I always loved about her." He glanced over at Ian. "I'm looking forward to seeing you out on the ice tonight. We have your dad in the owner's suite. I'm sure he'd love to see both of his boys score."

Ian tensed beside her but just mumbled something that sounded like "yes, sir." Then Jasper and Lucy took the executives-only elevator up to the owner's suite.

"The team owner used to be your stepdad?" Ian asked after the doors closed.

"Yup." And no one was more surprised than she was that he'd remembered her.

He rubbed the back of his neck as he gave her a considering look. "Seems like there's a lot about you that I don't know."

"Well, there's one way to fix that." Did that sound desperate? Did it matter?

Staring at the closed executive elevator doors, he gave one of his patented noncommittal grunts and walked into the locker room.

Annoyance and hurt singed every nerve from her toes upward. What a jackass. What had she been thinking? That things would be different? No. Not with Mr. I Don't Need to Say Anything.

He only wanted her when they were out of the tri-county metro area and they couldn't get enough of each other. That was dangerous. It was that makes-no-sense in-love-with-love territory her mom was always in. Everything was about the flash and the fire. Then, when that settled, she got bored and found a new husband. Out went Jasper and in came Andre and then Paul and then Scott. Shelby had seen firsthand the damage that type of instant ignition could have. That's why she'd known she had to keep Ian to just one night that turned into two. It couldn't be three. She was too sure she wasn't like her mom. She wouldn't bounce back. She'd fall with a splat. She already had.

...

Ian was trying to wrap his head around the idea of Shelby's former stepdad being Jasper fucking Dawson when he walked into the locker room and nearly slammed into a group of players circled around his dad.

He bit back a snarl, and it took longer than normal for him to get the locks in place holding down all that rage bubbling up underneath. By the time the other players went to dress, Ian was back in full control.

"Why are you here?" he asked.

His dad slapped him on the back as if he was in on the joke, the movement covering the fact that he was shoving Ian toward the door. "Can't a man come see his boys play the game he loves?"

With a quick maneuver, his old man got him back out into the hallway. Ian could have stopped it, but he was done walking away from this man. He was done having to keep the truth on lockdown. He was just 100 percent done.

"Cut to the chase," Ian said, looking his dad in the eyes. "What do you want?"

After a quick visual sweep of the hall to make sure they were alone, David leaned in and lowered his voice. "We need to do an interview. The three of us. Patch things up on national TV. It'll be good for you two, and it will lessen some of my negative exposure."

Ian laughed in his dad's face. "Negative exposure?"

"That's what my business partner is calling it." David focused his attention in short bursts on everything in the hallway except Ian. "I've sunk everything I have into a development outside of Toronto. Investors are getting worried by the bad press you two are causing."

"*We're* causing?" There wasn't even a hint of a whine of the metal on his mental locks under pressure; they burst open as if they'd never been there, and all those years of stuffing everything down came roaring up. "You're the one who had a secret second family."

His dad tensed and looked around before saying through his teeth, "Lower your voice."

Hands curled into fists, stance ready to throw down, blood rushing in his ears so loudly that his dad could be yelling right into his face and he wouldn't hear a thing, Ian pulled back, ready to let go with a vicious punch when the locker room door exploded outward. Alex strolled out as if all was right and good with the world, his body loose and his grin welcoming. He didn't stop until he was practically between Ian and their dad.

"Heya, Pops," Alex said. "I heard you'd come to visit."

David's face was bright red with fury. The man hadn't made it through the number of years in the professional hockey league that he had by not knowing when things were about to turn ugly. The catch was, there was no way he didn't realize he wouldn't come out on top.

"They're mine, you know," he snarled at Alex. "The records will always be mine. You may get close, but you'll never get there."

Alex shrugged as if he didn't give two shits about the records or anything the man in front of him could say. "I'd rather go scoreless for the rest of my career than to ever hold a record that had ever been connected to you."

"Who do you think you are?" he asked, emphasizing each word by jabbing his finger into Alex's chest.

Ian didn't think, he just reacted, grabbing his old man's hand and shoving it away. "He's my brother, and he doesn't have to take your shit." He took a step forward. He may be half the hockey player his dad was, but he was bigger, madder, and he had someone more important than himself to fight for. "Now get out of here before security comes for you."

He and Alex stood there, silent, shoulder to shoulder, and watched until David Petrov stormed out of the VIP door. For his entire life, after one of his father's "little lessons," he'd been left feeling completely alone.

This time was different.

"Brother, huh?" Alex asked, landing an elbow into Ian's side.

"Yeah, welcome to the family." Ian returned the nudge with a light shove of his own. "Don't forget to bring a side to Thanksgiving."

"I make a mean Jell-O salad with marshmallows and canned fruit."

Ian's taste buds revolted at the thought. "Crescent rolls might be more your speed."

They went into the locker room together, bickering back and forth like the old days, and it was like everything had fallen into place—almost.

As soon as the game was over, though, he was going to find Shelby.

Chapter Sixteen

After that brawl of a game, there was only one person Ian wanted to see, and it sure as hell wasn't the one reporters wouldn't stop asking him about. He'd made it two whole questions—both about his dad—into the postgame interviews before he bailed.

Now, here he was, sitting on the stoop outside Shelby's building like a sad puppy waiting for her to get home. He'd been there about half an hour when she came walking down the street with a guy in Cajun Rage gear.

What the hell?

Each of them was carrying the distinctive hot-pink cups that everyone in Harbor City recognized on the spot as being from the city's favorite LuLu's Pink Lemonade Cupcake Emporium. During the offseason, he ordered Uber Eats from there on the regular.

He stood up slowly, not wanting to scare her. He knew the moment she spotted him. Her steps faltered and her eyes rounded as an electric jolt of awareness shot between them, holding him to her steps as she drew nearer.

"Ian," she said, her gaze locked on him as a small, almost shy smile curled her lips. "What are you doing here?"

He was beyond the bullshit of coming up with some lame excuse. "Waiting for you."

Her smile deepened and her gaze dropped to the sidewalk as she fiddled with something in her pocket. He could watch her for hours, the way she rubbed her fingers over the short side of her hair when she was thinking things over, the snap in her eyes when she was giving him shit, the way she laughed, the sound escaping from her as if it were a surprise each time—all of it totally and completely Shelby.

So focused on drinking in every single aspect of her, Ian had nearly forgotten about the man with her until the guy cleared his throat and started talking.

"That was a helluva game. The last call really should have gone our way." He held out his hand to Ian. "Bill Henny. I'm with the Rage, and I've been trying to get Shelby here to switch teams, but she's pretty determined to stay with y'all."

Even the idea of her leaving Harbor City had him squeezing the other man's hand harder than necessary when they shook.

Shelby rolled her eyes and looked at the other man as if this were a conversation they'd had multiple times. "As much as I love you, Bill, I'm not gonna say yes."

"Our loss, Harbor City's gain." Bill checked his phone as a car with a Lyft sticker slowed down. "Looks like this is me. Next time you're in New Orleans, it's my turn to treat."

"Deal."

Standing side by side, Ian and Shelby watched the car drive away. It wasn't until it turned the corner at Towson Street that he realized they were holding hands. Being this close to her and not touching her had somehow become unnatural, no matter the zip code they were in.

He walked her up to her door, wishing with each step that

they were farther away so he could spend even that little extra amount of time with her. "Can I come in?"

Her sigh said so much without using a single word, but when she looked up at him, the light from the streetlamp highlighting her dark hair, there was no missing the way she looked at him as if she didn't want him to go, either. He had no idea how they'd gotten to this place of want-but-can't-have—it made no sense. Together, they made sense.

"We both know what will happen if you come in," she said, stepping nearer to him as if she couldn't help but be as close to him as possible. "I'm not sure if that's a good idea."

"Probably not." He glided his fingertips over the sensitive shell of her ear, relishing the way her breath hitched as desire darkened her eyes. "But after the game, you were the first person I wanted to see, the first one I wanted to talk to."

"Ian, that's not fair," she said, her voice breathy. "At the cabin, we agreed it would be once." She pressed her palm to his chest over his heart. "In the hotel, you were supposed to keep your hands in your pockets." She took a half step closer, eliminating any space between them as they stood touching, their faces close enough that they were practically kissing. "Now what's the limit we'll set?"

The temptation to dip his head just the smallest bit needed to complete the kiss was overwhelming, but this had to be her call. "Only when we beat the most hated team in Harbor City?"

She tugged her bottom lip between her teeth as she shook her head. "I should say no."

"I shouldn't even be here." But there was nowhere else in the world he'd rather be. Even if they never left this top step, if he was with Shelby, it felt right.

She took a quick step back, breaking contact between them and putting in the passcode on the building's security keypad. "Should we pretend you're just coming up for coffee?"

"I don't mind if we end up in the kitchen."

The kitchen, though, was exactly where they ended up. They rushed up the two flights of her walk-up, stopping to kiss every other step. It was nothing but hands everywhere, clothing being loosened, and anticipation riding high. They barely got in the front door before their clothes were coming off.

"You did say *kitchen*, right?"

He picked her up, carried her into her tiny kitchen, and sat her down on top of the table. Her shirt was halfway off and she made quick work of getting it the rest of the way gone.

His balls tightened at the sight of the high curves of her tits pushing against the black lace of her bra. The material gave just enough of a glimpse of her dusky pink nipples beneath to make pre-cum wet the tip of his dick.

"Are you okay if I fuck you long and hard right here in this kitchen?" He skimmed his hands down her sides before moving his fingers to the button of her black leather pants; then he popped it out, relishing the way her breath hitched. He pulled off her pants and dropped them on the floor, revealing a tiny scrap of lace that was the only thing covering her core. The sight gave him the perfect idea. "Lay back on the table, Shelby." He let out a hiss of a breath when she complied, spreading her legs as she did so. "Damn, you're so wet for me already, aren't you?"

She shot him a wicked grin. "Since I saw you sitting on my steps."

It could be her answer or the sight of her like that had him to yank down his jeans, pull her panties to the side, and drive straight and hard into her. Either way, she nearly squeezed the air out of his lungs. Something hungry and needy inside him demanded release to claim her, to make her his.

He didn't question it. Really, he didn't question anything

when it came to Shelby. The woman was different from anyone else he'd ever met. She didn't look at him and see the shadow of someone better. She saw him.

The center of her dark panties was several shades darker than the rest, and he breathed in the intoxicating scent of her arousal as he slid his thumb across her covered clit. She let out an appreciative moan and pushed her hips higher, pressing against his thumb.

"I love seeing you like this, so hot and ready." Ian slid the lace down her legs and dropped it to the floor.

He ran the backs of his knuckles across her exposed wet folds, so lightly that he was barely touching but more than enough to have both of them straining for more.

Her thighs trembled. "Fuck, Ian."

His cock twitched in anticipation. "That'll come later."

First he wanted to watch her ride that wave. He slid a finger into her entrance, circling it so it rubbed against every millimeter of her, slow and steady. Her thighs quivered and she lifted her hips in a silent plea for more.

"What do you want?" he asked.

She grabbed the edges of the table as if she had to anchor herself to reality. He understood the need exactly, except he was anchoring himself to her. Nothing felt more right than that. Forget one-night rules or zip-code requirements or anything else. This was where he belonged—with Shelby always.

"So slick. So soft. Let's see how you taste." The truth was, he couldn't wait any longer.

Lowering his mouth to her core, he lapped at her folds as she twined her fingers through his hair in encouragement. She didn't have to worry; he'd give her whatever she wanted. He glided his tongue across her clit, hard enough to push her to the edge but soft enough to leave her wavering on it without going over. Mouth, tongue, and fingers, he used them all to take her higher, to make her feel at this moment the way he felt about her every time he saw her—that rush of excitement and desire and something more that made being with her different. He couldn't explain it. He didn't understand it. He just needed her. Period.

· · ·

Shelby was on the edge. With each touch, each lick, the pleasure pulsed through her, She'd known it would be like this from their first kiss in the cabin—an almost desperate need for him and him alone. The electric vibrations in her thighs built higher and higher until her orgasm broke.

A blissful haze surrounded her, making any movement seem like it was beyond possibility, but she couldn't let it take over just yet. She needed more. She needed Ian. Sitting up, she looked at him standing between her legs, a lusty gleam darkening his eyes, his lips wet with her pleasure, and the clear outline of his hard cock visible against his jeans.

She got down from the table and reached behind her to unfasten her bra, slipping it off and dropping it to the floor. He, however, had too many clothes on. Without hesitation, she grasped the hem of his T-shirt and yanked it up, pulling it over his head, and tossing it away. Next, she went to work on his jeans, lowering the zipper, barely breathing as she did so, desperate to feel him.

Lowering herself to her knees as she took down his jeans and boxer briefs, she held her breath as his hard cock appeared, the tip wet with pre-cum. Some things weren't meant to be resisted. She licked and teased the head, sucking him into her mouth and relishing the resulting moan of appreciation. Then she took him deeper, teasing him with her tongue and sucking him hard as he rocked his hips in perfect rhythm with her mouth. It was so good how he filled her mouth. Even though she'd already come, her body was revving up for more, her core aching and desperate for Ian—only Ian.

Giving him one last lick, she looked up at him. "I need you inside me."

Eyes dark with desire, he sat down on the kitchen chair. "I'm here for whatever you want."

Best. Answer. Ever.

She swiped a condom from her purse and rolled it on his hard cock. Then, unable to wait any longer, beyond desperate for him, she braced her hands on his shoulders and lowered herself, taking him in completely in one long, torturously amazing stroke. He filled her, giving her exactly what she needed. He always did.

Ian wasn't hers, not the way she wanted him to be, but she couldn't deny him. Being with him was beyond dangerous, but she couldn't stop and didn't want to. She rocked against him on the downward thrust as her nails dug into his shoulders.

"That's it, Shelby," he said, his hands on her hips, lifting her and bringing her back down on him hard. "Take what you want."

It was all the encouragement she needed. She rocked against him, lifting herself up and down on his thick cock, losing herself in Ian. The closer she got to the edge, the more her body buzzed with an impending orgasm, the more she knew she wasn't lost. She'd finally found herself—not in him but with him.

She loved him.

Up and down, she undulated her hips, grinding against him on each downward stroke. Hard and fast, bordering on desperate, their bodies crashed together until she tossed her head back and came, groaning his name. He grasped her hips hard, moving her against him until he thrust upward one last time and came.

She collapsed against him, wrapping her arms around him as they sat in the chair, both breathing hard. Her clothes littered the floor from the front door to the table. His jeans were still on, just shoved all the way down to his ankles. The mail she'd brought in this morning and left on the table was scattered across the kitchen. Marv swam quick circles around his bowl on the counter, obviously in betta fish attack mode by the disturbance.

Ian Petrov had thrown her well-ordered life into chaos. Normally she'd hate that, but with him? It felt right. It felt perfect.

And that's what made her whole body clench. She'd fallen for the guy who thought of her as a fuck buddy. Sure, they got along and had fun hanging out, but they weren't dating—they hadn't even gone out on a date! This should just be pheromones in action, sexual attraction getting the best of them, having a good time. Instead, her heart had gotten involved—but not his.

How in the hell had she let this happen?

She got up and started gathering her clothes, the realization making her hands shaky and her breath quick. "I can't do this, Ian."

She thought she could. She had before. But with him, it was different. It mattered more—she should have realized it that night in the cabin in front of the fire. Whatever was between them, it wasn't one-night-stand material—at least not for her.

"Can't do what?" he asked as he dropped the condom in her trash and pulled up his pants.

She waved her hand between them. "This."

He stopped cold in the middle of her kitchen, and she watched as he transformed right before her eyes from the Ian she knew to the one who had faced off against the reporters. "I thought you were having fun."

Fun. That's all it was for him, and she knew this. They'd been up front from the beginning.

"It was amazing. *You're* amazing." But there was no way she could guard her heart against him. Really, it was too late for that. "I just can't."

He looked down at the tile floor and rubbed the back of his neck, the muscles in his jaw flexing. Tension flowed off him as he took a long, slow breath but when he lifted his head, there wasn't a single solitary expression on his totally neutral face.

Finally, he spoke, his voice low and gravelly. "I guess I'll go, then."

Her whole body ached as she stood there naked in her kitchen, her clothes pressed to her middle like a shield, as he put on his shirt and started toward the door. Biting the inside of her cheek to stop from crying, she inhaled a deep breath.

It had to be done. It would be worse the longer she let this go on. She knew all of that. It still hurt like she'd been dropped from the top of the Ice Knights arena.

He was halfway out the door before she got herself under control enough to talk. "I'm sorry."

He looked back at her, his jaw squared, his eyes focused on a spot over her left shoulder—but there was something in his eyes, a flash fight that gave her hope. She was walking toward him before she even realized it. Then it was gone and so was he, out the door, shutting it softly behind him.

And that's when the tears finally started to fall.

Chapter Seventeen

Putting on makeup before the team's annual skate with Harbor City's junior hockey athletes at Center Park rink had taken some extra time. Staying up half the night staring at the ceiling had given Shelby enough bags under her eyes for a two-week vacation. But when the emergency call had come in this morning that three of the staff scheduled to work the event had called in sick, of course she said yes, she'd help out.

Now she was standing in front of the rink door with Lucy, who was giving Shelby the rundown on her bouncer duties. It was chaotic, overwhelming, and the perfect activity for a day when she couldn't afford to let herself think about Ian and what could have been.

"Take this." Lucy handed her a clipboard with the guest list on it. "And this."

Shelby glanced down at the plastic squirt bottle Lucy held out. Okay, the guest list she got. This was a special event for the Ice Knights with a chance to meet and skate with all the grade-school-age skaters who played in the mini-mite games between periods to entertain the crowd. But a squirt bottle?

That she had no idea about.

Shelby took the bottle. "What's this for?"

"The park has a feral-cat problem, and for some reason they love the rink," Lucy said, scanning the crowd of reporters and photographers outside the arena like a general taking stock of opposing forces. "The last thing we need is for one of them to get in here, get freaked out by all the kids, and then take a swipe at little Mikey or Jenny."

"What's in it?"

"Just water, but it does the trick." She took a closer look at Shelby. "You doing okay?"

So much for her fine makeup skills. Who ever knew when to use the green cover-up or the peach cover-up or the dark brown?

"I'm amazing," Shelby said, putting enough fake cheer in her tone to be a Christmas commercial. "Totally excited to be a part of this."

"You are the worst liar I've ever met," Lucy said with a disbelieving chuckle. "Okay, well, no one who's not on the list can gain access—not even Wayne Gretzky. No press. No nothing. This one-on-one time with the kids is a sacred event for the Ice Knights."

An hour later, the rush of kids and their parents had slowed and she finally had time to scan the area for attack kitties and pretend she wasn't spending every other breath thinking about Ian. She'd made the right decision to cut things off completely, even if it made her feel like shit—at least that's what she kept telling herself to squelch all the maybe-I-could or if-only-I-did thoughts swirling around her head and making her heart ache.

"Hey, Stacey, right?" David Petrov strolled up to the entrance flanked by two guys with press badges around their necks.

"Shelby," she said, more than used to people mixing up

her name that way.

"Oh man. Sorry about that. Too many hits to the noggin." With an amused chuckle, he tapped the top of his head with his knuckles. "Don't suppose you can let me inside to go find my boys."

Her gut twisted. The man was obviously trying to make amends with Alex and Ian. She could understand how hard that was and admired his determination to set things right, but a skate with fifth graders may not be the time to do it—especially with Lucy's instructions.

"I'm afraid I can't do that." If Wayne Gretzky couldn't get in, David Petrov couldn't, either. "It's just for the junior athletes and the team. I can let them know and they can call you after it's over?"

"It'll be quick." He took a step forward as if to barrel past her. "Believe me, no one loves the little players like I do."

"I wish I could, but I can't." She took a quick step to the left, blocking his path forward. Ugh. She hated having to do this, but she didn't have a choice or another option. There had to be a way to buy some time or distract him with another possibility—*oh wait!* "What if I could set up a dinner with the three of you for after the event? I mean, I can't guarantee it or anything, but—"

"Aren't you a doll to think of arranging a dinner between a father and his boys," he said, a snide, patronizing timbre sneaking in under his tone. "I still need to get in there now, though. These reporters came all the way from Toronto to talk to the three of us."

Ian plus a surprise visit from his dad and reporters? That would go nuclear fast. "I'm sorry, but I can't."

He shot a don't-worry-about-it smile at the Canadian reporters, but when he turned back to her, his face was hard and angry.

"Which one of my sons are you fucking?" he asked, his

voice quiet and mean. "Is it Ian or Alex? I hope you're smart enough to snag Alex. He's more talented by about a zillion and he'll have the endorsements. More money to be had that way. You're a smart girl; you can see what I'm leading to, can't you?"

Like he was wearing a neon sign saying puck bunny, but it didn't make sense. He was here to make amends, a little fatherly twelve-step program. That was the only reason she could even fathom for all of this. He was David Petrov. The hockey world revered him. He was a good man who'd made a mistake. That's what he'd told the world and everyone had believed him—*she'd* believed him.

"Look, Shelly," he said with enough emphasis on her name to broadcast that he was getting it wrong on purpose. "Walk me inside to my boys right now or I'll work it so Alex breaks up with you." His eyes narrowed. "Shit. It's Ian, isn't it? You're not bright at all. That boy doesn't have it. I told him when he was young, but he thought hard work would be enough. It isn't. This league chews up and spits out players like him all the time. He's not worth your time."

And that's what it took to snap her out of her shock that David the Great was a total and complete asshole. Not worth her time? Ian was worth that and so much more.

"How dare you," she said, emotion pushing her voice up to the squeak ranges. "He's your son."

He snorted. "I'm in the Hall of Fame; he'll be lucky to last another year. He'll never be another me."

Fury at this man's absolute callousness toward Ian set her blood on fire and the words flew out. "Thank God, because that means instead of a narcissistic asshole, he's a good man who holds babies when they're fussy, who volunteers to drive down a snow-packed mountain rather than let someone with bald tires do it, and who thinks more about other people than himself. He's a million times a better man than you could even imagine."

By the time she was done, her face was hot, her chest was heaving, and her heart was going a million miles an hour, powered by adrenaline, love for a man she couldn't have, and fury at the man who'd toss him aside.

"Nice speech," David said, sounding bored. "Are you going to let me in or do I need to call up Jasper?"

She crossed her arms, never more confident in her life that things were going to go her way. "Go ahead."

He took out his phone, as smug as only a complete jerk like him could be. "Jasper. I hate to tell you this, but I'm having a problem with one of your employees. I think you need to set her straight. Yeah, her name is Shelby... Yeah, that's the one." His face turned red. "What? Fuck me? Are you kidding? Do you know who I am?" He paused and then brought his phone down to look at the screen, jaw open in shock. "He hung up on me."

Thank you, Jasper Dawson, for being the best former stepdad in the world.

David glared at her. "You no-good squeaky bitch, you're going to pay."

She didn't think. She didn't strategize. She just reacted, grabbing the water bottle and spraying one of hockey's most revered players in the face—repeatedly—while photographers documented the entire exchange, their flashes going off in quick succession. Like he was a bad cat. The fact that he sort of hissed at her as he stomped off kind of helped with that mental picture.

And to think that Ian had grown up with that man and that people actually tried to compare him to that awful jerk. She sucked in a sharp breath as realization struck. The place was surrounded by press, and someone was going to tell him if he didn't see it on the news himself. He'd hate that. There was nothing he hated more than being in the middle of a media feeding frenzy and she sure had just started one.

She had to go find Ian.

• • •

Ian was helping to show a player how he taped up his stick when he realized that at least half the kids and most of the parents were looking out the windows toward the park.

He looked down at Jorge, a ten-year-old version of himself—a little slower than the other players and slap shot not as hard, but with that same big-hearted love of the game. "What's going on?"

"David Petrov is here," the kid said. "Everyone's going to see him."

Ian looked out the front window, which gave him the perfect viewpoint to see his dad laying on the charm thick. Shelby was smiling. The two guys with his dad had the kind of cameras and microphones that only reporters have. He fiddled with the window and got it open in time to hear her offer up him and Alex as dinner dates for his dad.

His gut dropped. There wasn't any point in listening to more.

He'd spent the entire night trying to work out why she'd kick him to the curb without explanation, but the pieces had fallen together nicely. He'd become a dead end in her quest.

Their conversation when they'd been on the team jet about a staged dinner replayed in his head. He'd been crystal clear about the fact that he wasn't going to do that. Ever. Now she was making the suggestion to his dad, who was the bigger media get. Part of the allure of David Petrov was his unwillingness to speak to the press. The regular fans thought it was because he was one of them, a no-bullshit everyman. The truth was because even his old man knew he couldn't keep up the pretense of being a good person if people started asking questions. That made an interview with David Petrov—especially the first one with both his sons—the ultimate career maker.

Shelby had ambition and smarts. It wasn't just anyone who could create a hockey juggernaut like The Biscuit from nothing and then make a deal with hockey's biggest club to make it the cornerstone of their media empire. He was twelve kinds of an idiot for not seeing it until now. Even the fact that she never brought it up was a clue—she wouldn't want him to think of her as a member of the press.

With what felt like battery acid sloshing around in his stomach, he shut the window and went back to skate around the ice with Jorge. Needing the distraction and tapping into that coaching side of himself that always leveled out his emotions, Ian showed the kid a few tricks to get his speed up a little.

Jorge had a ton of heart. That tended to be just as important as the talent once a player got to the more elite levels. There were plenty of great players out there who didn't want to put in the work or got burned out. Those heart players, though, they kept the team together.

After finishing up with Jorge, he made his way to the locker room, determined to get the hell out of here before the closing press conference that would only lead to questions about his dad, their relationship, and every other personal thing that he tried to keep private while living under the microscope he'd grown up beneath.

He had most of his stuff in his bag when the locker room door flew open and Shelby hurried in, relief clear on her face the moment she spotted him. It was a kick in the gut and it took everything he had not to flinch.

Oh yeah, wouldn't want to miss out on your chance to make reservations.

"Ian," Shelby said, hurrying over. "I've been looking for

you."

He just bet she had.

"To ask me to go to dinner with the old man?" he asked without bothering to look up as he loaded his stuff faster, zipping it with more force than necessary. "Did you manage to work out that you'd get to publish the post on The Biscuit?"

She jolted to a stop, concern bringing her eyebrows together as she twisted up her mouth. "What are you talking about?"

He slung the bag over his shoulder and took a long look at the woman he'd fallen for. He really was a class-A fool. She looked exactly the same—like the woman who'd made him think things could be different. But she was the same as everyone. It was all about his connection to David the Great.

"I heard you make the plan with him," he said, starting toward the door.

She clasped her hands in front of her belly and exhaled a long breath. "I was trying to buy time, to keep him from rushing in here with those two reporters because I knew you wouldn't want to have to deal with that."

He stopped walking. Best to get this all out now. He'd spent too much of his life covering for other people's shit motives.

"Yeah, never mind that a story like this could help you renegotiate your contract with the Ice Knights," he said, the words coming out raw from that part of him that made him a heart player on the ice. It was the part that hoped, that believed, that burned for more—at least it had been. "Really, getting the three of us together—well, David the Great who never gives interviews for sure—would help solidify your career trajectory and your importance in the Ice Knights media plan."

It all made perfect sense, but he still didn't want to believe it. There was no other explanation, though—after all, she'd been the loud mouth who leaked the story about his parentage in the first place.

"That is so much bullshit," Shelby said, her voice shaking with anger.

All of that show was probably a mix of guilt and shame at getting caught. He had no time for it.

"You'd have the one story no one else could get and all you had to do to get it was worm your way into my life." He white-knuckled his grip on his bag at the realization that hit. "Tell me, the cabin. Was it really an accident? Did you give the house marker a little extra kick to have it read six instead of nine? You were there before me. You easily could have done it for the hockey story of the year."

She jerked back as if he'd slapped her. Then she straightened, her chin lifting as she looked at him as if he was the one who'd betrayed her.

"Are you ever not the victim in a situation?"

That was fucking laughable. As if he was just feeling sorry for himself. "Excuse me?"

She marched over to him, her steps eating up the distance at a sharp, quick clip. "I understand your life hasn't been easy, but when are you going to stop assuming that the only reason anyone wants you or thinks about you is because you're David Petrov's kid?"

"That is the only reason people are interested." He'd accepted it years ago. It was what it was. There was no point in fighting it.

"You are so full of shit." Her hands were on her hips and her face was flush with emotion. "Hundreds of thousands of kids hit the ice thinking that maybe they can make it to the NHL one day. Only a few hundred actually wear the professional jersey each season. Do you really think you got your spot because of your last name?"

"It got me a look." Coaches had told him exactly that

straight to his face.

Shelby let out a frustrated sigh. "Yeah, you're right. You had an advantage for sure, but it's not the only reason you're here. There are a lot of hockey players' kids out there who never made it to this level."

"They weren't David Petrov's kid." His dad was a legend. A hockey god. The kind who kids everywhere pretended to be.

"For someone who is so fucking concerned that everyone only sees him as his father's kid, it sure looks to me like the only one who does is you." She crossed her arms, challenging him with her straight-on glare. "It's time for you to grow up and decide. Are you David Petrov's kid or are you Ian Petrov, your own man?"

The punch landed harder than a check against the glass, laying him out right there for the world to see.

"I'm gone, that's who I am."

And he walked out the door, got into his car, and kept driving until Harbor City wasn't even a glimmer in his rearview mirror.

Chapter Eighteen

Ian hadn't meant to end up back at the cabin, but here he was. He didn't have any bags. He'd driven up the snow-free mountain roads, the wildflowers starting to peek through the spring grass, and had pulled into the driveway just as the Morgans were adding an Airbnb rental sign to the brand-new address plaque.

He parked and walked over to Mrs. Morgan, who was supervising Mr. Morgan as he used the post hole digger. "Can I rent it today?"

Mrs. Morgan smiled in recognition. "You betcha, especially since you're a big reason why we decided to list it."

Ten minutes later—after he'd helped Mr. Morgan finish putting up the sign—he was touring the cabin with Mrs. Morgan as if he hadn't been there before. He'd sat at that table eating his oatmeal when Shelby had told him about how the news that Alex was his brother had slipped out. He'd walked up those stairs to the bedroom the first night and had found Shelby armed with a Taser and ready to take on a burglar. That rug was the one she'd lay back on, gorgeous and naked.

What in the hell was he doing here?

Mrs. Morgan looked up at him with concern. "Are you sure you're okay, honey?"

"I'm fine." He tried to smile. Judging by the way she scrunched up her face and took a half step back, he didn't quite make it happen. "Thanks for letting me rent the place."

"And your friend?" Mrs. Morgan asked. "She's not coming?"

He shook his head. Just the idea of her being in Harbor City while he was here should be a relief. It wasn't. Instead, it hurt like a motherfucker.

"That's too bad. I liked her." Mrs. Morgan made a *tsk-tsk* sound. "Well, the electricity is back up and the cell people brought a new tower online, so service is a lot better. Oh, and we found that bottle of scotch of yours in the bedroom. I meant to send it to you but just kept forgetting. Looks like that worked out, though." She started walking toward the door, still talking a mile a minute. "Our granddaughter is acting as the maid for the foreseeable future after what she pulled with using this as a party house, so if you need any messes cleaned up, you let me know."

"I'll be fine on my own."

The words came out harsher than he meant, and Mrs. Morgan jerked to a stop, giving him an assessing look. "I'm sure you will be, but there's no harm in changing your mind."

He nodded as if those were some deep, prophetic words and walked her to the door. As soon as the SUV with all the Morgans packed inside pulled onto the highway, Ian opened the bottle of scotch and poured two fingers' worth into a juice glass. He carried it over to the couch and stared at the unlit fireplace.

He was three drinks in, still sitting in silence staring at the empty grate, when his cell rang. Like an asshole, he answered without checking the caller ID first.

"Where in the hell are you?"

"Hello to you, too, Dad."

The other man grumbled something under his breath. "Where are you?"

"In Buffly County." It was a big place and he had no intention of giving his dad any more specifics than that.

"What in the hell are you doing way up there? Are you with that woman?" He let out a long sigh. "Ian, you can find a woman anywhere. There is no reason to deal with one who doesn't have your best options in mind."

He set his half-empty glass of scotch down on the coffee table, unease taking away that soft fuzziness the alcohol had given him. "What are you talking about?"

"She wouldn't let me in to that stupid event with the dumb kids. She wouldn't guarantee a dinner. She just wants to interfere, to come between us. You're better off without her."

For as much as he wanted to believe his dad was lying, he knew deep in his gut that he was actually telling the truth—not about being better off without her but about her actions at the rink. She'd tried to tell him. He hadn't listened. His brain had automatically gone to that place it had always gone. Years of his dad comparing Ian to him had left a mark so deep, he hadn't even realized just how bad it was.

You'll never skate like I did.

That kid only wants to hang out with you because of me.

That coach was doing me a favor when he called to see if you were interested in playing.

You'll never be the player I was.

All of it had never been about Ian. It had only been about his dad and his ego. Without realizing, Ian had fallen into that habit, looking at every part of his life only in comparison to his dad's.

The mental locks he'd built up over decades of having

to deal with his dad were hanging useless and busted. He braced himself for that explosion of rage. It didn't come. Oh, there was anger and annoyance and the kind of fuck-me-are-you-serious irritation that had him clamping his jaw shut tight enough to give him a headache, but no lights-out rage. Whatever was coming for his dad, none of it mattered anymore.

Oblivious to Ian's silence, David kept talking, "No son of mine will…"

The rest of his words faded out, replaced by Shelby's question. Who was Ian? He sure as hell wasn't this man's son. He didn't have to live up to David Petrov's scoring records or on-ice skills. He never had. He was Ian fucking Petrov and he had better shit to do than to listen to an egomaniac rant about how he was done wrong.

Nothing he could do or say would change his dad. The only thing he could do was kick him out of his life for good.

So he hung up without saying a word because it wouldn't have made any difference, deleted the old man's contact information, and blocked him.

That took care of one problem in his life but left a bigger one. How in the hell was he going to fix this with Shelby?

He had no fucking clue.

• • •

Shelby's whole life was about to change. This morning she'd woken up, called Bill, and told him that if the offer was still open, she'd love to come to New Orleans.

Love.

If she'd been an idiot to fall in love with a man who not only didn't feel the same but actually thought she was some kind of media double agent, then maybe she could transfer all of that to her work. Hockey had saved her before; it could save her again. It had to.

Now she had to give the hardest goodbye.

Dressed all in black, Shelby fit right in with the crowd at The Black Hearts art gallery for Roger's latest show—well, except for the deep-pockets part. These people weren't just suburban rich, they were straight-up own-a-good-chunk-of-the-city rich, like the Beckett cousins who were trying to outbid each other on Roger's models, no doubt just to say they'd won if the tabloid stories about them were right.

Tonight was the first time she'd been out of her house except for work since the fight with Ian. It wasn't like she was sitting at home with a pint of ice cream and sad songs cued up on Spotify. Okay, the melodramatic-ballad part was totally true. She was spending her time checking out restaurants in New Orleans. Bill hadn't been lying. There were a ton of places she'd love to try out. In some ways that made her decision easier—at least that's what she was telling herself.

She was standing in front of a gorgeous painting of a nude model in the back of the gallery when Roger found her. He handed her a glass of ginger ale with a slice of lime in it.

"How's your motor running?" he asked.

She pursed her mouth to keep her emotions at bay. Damn. She was going to miss these little chats. "Not well."

He took her arm and led her to a quiet corner near a Hudson painting and used his most *Leave It to Beaver* voice. "Tell Roger everything."

It was just what she needed to make her chuckle. "You know it's weird when you talk about yourself in the third person."

"These rich people eat it up." He looked over at the people walking around the gallery checking out his models. "They think it makes me sound more artistic and they pay higher prices for it."

"I'm going to miss you so badly." Understatement of the

century.

He tilted his head to the side. "Where am I going?"

"You're not. I am." She took a deep breath and let it out slowly, doing her best to ignore that twinge in her gut warning she was making a mistake. The decision was made. She just had to stick to it. "I'm going to New Orleans tomorrow. The Cajun Rage offered me a deal I'd be a fool to walk away from, but the catch is that I have to start right away."

"Is this because of that hockey player?"

"No." She fiddled with her six-year coin in her jacket pocket. "Why would you think that?"

He chuckled and shook his head. "Because I know you."

And that was the thing about a good sponsor—and a good friend—they always did. She'd have better luck lying to herself than to Roger. "I love him."

"You'd think that would be a reason to stay."

She blinked back the tears that pricked her eyes. "He doesn't love me, and even if he did, he's not at the right place in his life for that. He's got some stuff he needs to work out. The fresh start will do me good."

They hugged, putting six years' worth of ups and downs, triumphs and tragedies into one huge squeeze.

"You'll always be my favorite Mustang."

She swallowed over the lump of emotion clogging her throat. "Love you right back, Roger."

Another quick hug and she hustled out of the gallery before she started crying. She'd never imagined leaving Harbor City. It was her place. However, she couldn't turn around without seeing something Ice Knights related and she just couldn't deal with that. Maybe in a few years she'd come back, but she couldn't deal with it now.

A text buzzed on her phone confirming her Uber to the airport tomorrow. That was a good thing, right? She was moving on to bigger and better things. She could learn to love a new city and a new team. As for learning to love another man, she hoped she never did that ever again.

...

The sun was barely up when someone started pounding on the cabin door. If Ian had been asleep—or had fallen asleep at all—he would have been pissed. As it was, he was half in the bag and staring blankly at the now-roaring fire when the knocking started. He ignored it, but it didn't stop. There was only one person he knew who was that obnoxious and he wasn't going to stop until Ian answered.

The room didn't spin when he stood up, which meant he needed more scotch. Still, he took his time getting to the door. It was the least he could do to be equally annoying.

His brother didn't wait to be asked in; he just pushed his way past Ian and into the living room.

"Why is is hotter than hell in here?" Alex asked, pulling at the collar of his shirt.

"I started a fire." Something that was totally obvious to him and he'd been drinking.

Alex looked from the fire to Ian. "Why?"

"Because there needed to be one." And because it reminded him of Shelby, just like absolutely everything including breathing. "What are you doing here?"

"Coming to get you before you throw a complete and total pity party." He looked around. "You haven't started single Adele yet, have you?"

"She's amazing." He flipped off his brother and then flopped back down on the couch. "How did you find me?"

"Dad called."

Of course. He grabbed his glass of scotch, the same one he'd been nursing for the entire night. "Did you tell him to fuck off?"

"What do you think?" *Translation: Abso-fucking-lutely.* Alex swiped his glass and carried it over to the kitchen sink, where he dumped it. "Let's go, I'm taking you to the airport."

The fuck? They didn't have a game for two more days thanks to the length of that epic road trip. He was going to spend at least the next twenty-four hours sitting here in this hell-hot room and finishing the bottle of scotch. "I'm not going anywhere."

Alex walked back to the living room, where he started to put out the fire. "She's leaving."

He didn't have to ask who. There was only one "she" in his life.

"She's going to New Orleans," Alex continued. "Lucy said she's going to start up a media content center for the Rage."

If he had anything other than alcohol in his stomach at that moment, he would have thrown it up. Instead, he set his jaw and reached for the bottle of scotch on the coffee table. He'd just have to drink until he could puke and maybe that would numb the pain shooting through him.

He took a swig straight from the bottle, relishing the burn all the way down to his gut. "Good for her."

"Are you fucking kidding?" Alex glared at him. "That's your reaction?"

"Why, because she's going to support our biggest rival?" He took another drink, wondering how long it would take before he forgot what Alex had just said.

"No, you idiot." Alex stormed over and grabbed the scotch from Ian's grasp. "Because you love her."

"I don't love her." And if he said it enough, he'd start to believe himself. Shit. What had he done? "I fucked it all up."

"You have the drive back to Harbor City to figure out how to fix it." Alex yanked Ian up off the couch and shoved him toward the door. "Come on. You don't have time to waste. You're paying the speeding tickets, though."

Ian tried to process that. "You drove all the way out here just to drive me back?"

"Yeah." Alex looked at him as if he was the dumbest person in the world. "It's what brothers do."

There wasn't anything he could say to that. The beauty of it was, though, he didn't need to. Instead, he nodded at Alex and his brother rolled his eyes at him in return. No translation needed.

If only figuring out what he was going to say to Shelby would be as easy.

Chapter Nineteen

The car was barely at a stop near the airport curb before Ian had the door open. Thanks to a call to Lucy, he'd gotten Shelby's flight information and the tip that she liked to get to the airport two hours in advance. Of course she did. She carried around a flashlight Taser; she didn't leave anything to chance. He glanced down at the clock on his phone screen. He was cutting it beyond close.

"Thanks, Alex," he said as he got out. "I couldn't have done it without you."

"No shit," his brother responded. "Now go fix your fuckup."

Ian sprinted through the airport doors and through the crowd at the airport. He deked left and then right, making his way toward the security gates where a crowd of people waited in lines that barely seemed to move. It was as far as he could go without a ticket. There were two hours before her flight. She had to be here.

He jumped up on a trio of seats off to the side and scanned the crowd looking for Shelby. Trying to find one person in the room of wall-to-wall people was like trying to find a guy without a mullet in an eighties hockey video montage.

"Shelby Blanton!" he hollered, his heart hammering in his ears.

People turned and looked around, glad for some entertainment while they waited. Several training their phones on him, no doubt to send the video of the Harbor City weirdo at the airport to their friends back in Omaha. A few TSA agents turned in his direction and started toward him. He didn't give a shit.

"Shelby, I know you're mad and you have every right to be." This was where that whole grunts-more-than-talks thing became a problem. When he needed the words, he didn't know what to say. So he went with the first thing that came to mind. "I was an asshole." Wow. He really should have made a plan, but it was too late to now. "I don't have the right to ask, but I'm asking for another chance in every zip code. Please."

"Sir," one of the TSA agents said. "I'm gonna need you to get down from there."

Fuck. "Just one minute more?"

The agent pulled out a pair of zip ties. "Depends on how curious you are about the inside of the airport jail. Stay up there and you'll get the full tour."

If it would mean seeing Shelby, he would have happily taken the arrest option, but nowhere in the crowd was a tall, dark-haired woman ready to tell him he was a dumbass and then hopefully forgive him.

"Flight six twenty to New Orleans, do you know if it got delayed?" he asked, still eyeballing the passengers in line, looking for Shelby.

The agent shook his head. "Some kind of storm system is moving through later, so they moved up that flight's departure time. Turned this place into chaos with all those passengers trying to get through early. It has already boarded and is about to take off. You're too late."

The news was a punch in the gut that knocked all the air out of him. He flopped down into the chair, his legs not strong enough to hold him up under the staggering weight of the news.

"I heard a rumor, though, that they added another flight out tonight to make up for it," the agent said.

It was the best news he'd ever heard. Whatever it took, he was getting on that flight.

• • •

Sitting in seat 14C on a plane destined for New Orleans, Shelby tightened the seat belt.

Then she loosened it.

Then she tightened it again.

No matter what she did, though, it felt wrong, but then again so did everything. Packing up her belongings and sticking the boxes in the building's basement storage until she found a place in New Orleans made her eye twitch. Putting her carry-on stuffed with a week's worth of clothes in the overhead bin made her queasy. The Ice Knights home screen on her phone made her weepy.

And the idea that Ian was out there somewhere and that she wouldn't see him again? That was fucking terrifying.

Every nerve in her body was screaming and her fight-or-flight response had gone to full-on get-the-hell-out-of-here mode. All she could think of was Ian. The night he taught her how to skate. How he'd stuck up for his brother even when he was so mad, he couldn't talk to Alex. The breathtaking way he looked at her after making her come so hard she was surprised her toes weren't still curled.

She had to get out of here.

She had to get to Ian.

On the verge of hyperventilating, she unfastened her seat belt and stood up. On the inhale, she popped open the overhead bin and on the exhale, she had her bag and was heading down the aisle as the other passengers stared at her and wondered aloud what was going on.

She'd made it almost to the front when a flight attendant blocked her way.

"The cabin doors are about to close," he said with a testy smile. "You have to sit down."

"I need to get out of here." She had to get to Ian.

"Ma'am." The flight attendant straightened his glasses and gave her an imperious glare. "We'll be taking off soon."

Yeah, that was exactly why her heart was going a bazillion miles an hour, her brain was in full panic mode, and she had been rushing toward the jetway. "I understand, just let me off before you do." She paused, gathering up all the fear and hope for what was going to happen next and putting it into the most important word. "Please."

The flight attendant's demeanor changed in an instant and he ushered Shelby to the front of the plane. "Is everything okay? Do you require assistance?"

She shook her head. The only person who could get her out of this mess was herself, but help with Harbor City traffic would be appreciated. "Not unless you can get me a cab and through rush-hour traffic to the Ice Knights arena in less than an hour."

He raised both eyebrows so high, they got lost behind his perfectly coiffed hair and gestured toward the walkway. "You'd need a miracle for that."

"Then that's what I have to hope for." And she took off down the jetway, knowing she was probably on a fool's mission, but she had to try.

She loved Ian Petrov and if there was a chance—even a small one—for a happily ever after with the sexy, grunting, stubborn man with enough family baggage to fill a 747, then she had to try.

Hustling down the jetway, she regretted every step of the way that she'd decided to wear heels. She barely made it to the gate before she took them off and started sprinting for real, the tiny wheels on her cheap carry-on making the case bounce and swerve as she ran.

The TSA agent sitting at the checkpoint between the secured and not-secured area stood up as Shelby neared and eyed her suspiciously as she moved to block her exit. "Ma'am, I'm gonna need you to slow down."

Getting arrested for causing an airport disturbance was the last thing she needed right now, but when a person figured out what needed to happen next so they could start the rest of their life, they wanted it to start now.

"I'm sorry." Shelby held up the hand with her black heels. "I just have to get out of here as fast as possible."

The agent put her hand up to the walkie-talkie on her shoulder, body language loose but ready to rumble. "Why do you have to do that?"

How in the hell was she supposed to explain what had happened with Ian in the shortest amount of time so she could get out of the airport, hail a cab, and get her ass to the Ice Knights arena? There was no fucking way, but she had to try.

Coming to a stop six feet away from the TSA agent, Shelby sucked in a deep breath, ready to get it all out as quickly as possible when she looked over the agent's shoulder and spotted Ian on the other side of the do-not-cross line.

All the adrenaline pumping through her system vanished in an instant. He was here. Ian Petrov was at the airport. He'd come after her. "I have to go tell that man right there that I love him."

The agent looked over at Ian and then back at Shelby and

what she could only assume was the 100 percent over-the-top goofy grin on her face. Shaking her head, the agent walked back over to her chair.

"I have been waiting years for this to happen." She sat down. "Go ahead, honey, I'll be rooting for you."

Shelby wanted to, but all of a sudden, her feet stopped working. All she could do was stand there with her shoes in one hand and the handle of her suitcase in the other, looking at the man she loved and trying to figure out what to say.

Ian looked like hell. His hair was going every which way, as if he hadn't been able to stop ramming his hands through it; he had at least two days' worth of beard growth; and he was pacing back and forth while talking animatedly to someone on the phone.

"What do you mean, there aren't any open seats tonight for a flight to New Orleans?" He let his head fall back as he grimaced. "It's a major tourist destination—there has to be at least one spot."

"Why are you going to New Orleans?" Shelby asked from her side of the do-not-cross line.

Ian spun around, his eyes wide, and hung up his phone without saying goodbye to whomever was on the other line.

"I have to tell you something," he said, looking at her with such love in his eyes that she nearly melted right there on the spot. "But I still don't know what to say."

• • •

Okay, he'd royally fucked that up. Could he make this any worse? Well, considering she was staying on her side of the do-not-cross line, probably not.

She was looking at him like he'd lost his mind and maybe he had—the idea of never being with her again did that to him.

"Do you want to go somewhere more private?" she asked without moving from her spot.

He looked over at all the people in the security line, and everyone was watching. By now most of them had their phones out, recording, and there was no missing the chattering about who he was. All of this would be on social media in minutes if it wasn't being live broadcast already. Normally this was exactly the time when he'd walk away, get out of the spotlight as fast as he could, but he wouldn't risk walking away from Shelby ever again. Being with her was worth whatever judgment came down from the Harbor City sports media, fans, and anyone else. The only person's opinion besides his own that he cared about was Shelby's.

He had no idea what to say to fix his fuckup, but he knew the most important part. "I love you."

She dropped the shoes she was holding and lost her grasp on her suitcase. "What?"

"I know," he said. "I was surprised, too."

Her eyes rounded and a loud "ooooooooh" went up from the crowd. The older woman in the TSA uniform on the other side of the do-not-cross line rolled her eyes as she shook her head.

"Wait." He held up his hand and prayed like hell that Shelby wouldn't just walk away. "That came out wrong. Fuck me, this is why I don't talk." He took a deep breath and tried again. "I didn't plan to fall in love with you, but really I should have expected the unexpected when it came to you after you Tased me in the cabin."

Another "oooooohhhh" from the crowd grew louder, and with everyone recording, there was no way that part wouldn't end up on the news. *Way to go, Petrov.* "She thought I was a burglar who'd broken in—it was totally justified."

Satisfied she wouldn't end up arrested for assault, he focused back on Shelby. "You're funny and smart and you push me when I need it. I know you don't love me, but I'm hoping you'll give me a chance, that you'll at least be open to the idea of dating and seeing if your feelings change. I think it could really work out."

Her chin was wobbling and her voice shaky, but there was no misunderstanding what she said next. "You couldn't be more wrong."

Her statement hit him like a Mack truck followed by a herd of water buffalo in mid-stampede.

"I do love you," she said.

Shock didn't begin to cover it. More like what-a-pair-of-jerks-they-were.

"That's why I had to tell you we couldn't…" She glanced over at the crowd, her cheeks turned pink, and she focused back on him. "Well, we couldn't anymore. I was afraid that I would just keep falling more in love with you and you'd leave me with a broken heart."

He crossed right up to the do-not-cross line, not stopping until he was right in front of her. "I'd never do that."

"But, Ian," she said, her eyes watery. "You did."

And he'd spend the rest of his life making up for it if that's what it took. "I was an idiot with his head shoved way too far up his ass. I removed it. I promise: I'll be with you if we're ever arrested for trespassing again, go ice-skating, make out in the owner's suite, or just sitting on the couch talking smack about the hair of the players in whatever classic hockey game is on."

He glanced over at the TSA agent by the podium and raised an eyebrow in question. She smiled and waved her hand.

Crossing that line was like walking into a new future, one that he couldn't wait to start. He pulled her into his arms, dipping his head down to kiss her but stopping just shy of her lips. "I love you, Shelby Blanton."

"I love you, too." Then she raised herself up on her toes and kissed him, soft, promising, and forever.

Somewhere in the background he heard whistles, claps, and hollers, but he couldn't be bothered. He had Shelby in his arms and there was absolutely nothing in the world more important than that.

Epilogue

Three years later...

The Pikeville Thundercats were still celebrating their AHL championship victory at a scaled-down hometown parade when Ian got the call. Not that he knew it at the time. He'd taken one look at his phone screen, seen Jasper's name, and handed it off to Shelby. She handed it right back after answering it.

Now here he was trying to hear the Ice Knights owner over the sound of the crowd cheering the minor league players and process what he'd just said. "I'm sorry, can you repeat that?"

Jasper Dawson yelled loud enough that the astronauts in the space station probably heard, "I said, we want to bring you in. Coach Peppers is starting to eye retirement and we want to bring in someone who knows our system to serve as assistant coach and then, in a year or two, head coach."

He glanced over at Shelby, who was playing peekaboo with one of the Thundercat players' babies while swaying back and forth with their eight-month-old on her hip. He had a great life here. He was coaching kids and doing his best to win games and get his players to the big time. Shelby worked remotely for the Ice Knights and drove around a classic Mustang outfitted with all the most modern safety gear (a wedding gift from Roger). They'd made their place in Pikesville, and going back to Harbor City was something he hadn't even hoped to have happen for another ten years.

"Are you sure?" Ian asked.

"Peppers said there's no one he could imagine doing a better job," Dawson said. "You are our first choice and not just because you're Ice Knights family. We've been watching you with the Thundercats. We know you're capable of amazing things. So what do you say?"

He caught Shelby's eye. She was already giving him a thumbs-up and mouthing, *Say yes*. Of course she'd already known; she did have an inside track to the team.

"Yes."

"Great, now hand me back over to Shelby. I want to hear all about how that grandson of mine is doing."

Ian glanced down at the dark-haired kid in her arms. "He's crashed out at the victory celebration. I guess he likes the noise."

Dawson chuckled."Well then, little Alex is going to love Harbor City."

Later, after the team celebration was over and the baby was tucked into bed, he and Shelby sat down in front of the fire burning on one of the static TV channels—it was June, after all.

"What do you think of going to Harbor City and house hunting sometime soon?" They'd need to find a place with a yard for Alex to play in and an extra room for baby number two who they were already planning.

"On one condition," she said, snuggling in closer to him

on the couch.

"What's that?"

"A visit to the cabin first." She kissed her way up his neck. "My mom has volunteered to run Camp Grandma for the week."

Buying the actual number six house next door to the Morgans had been one of their first investments as a couple and one of his favorites. "I'll make sure the sheriff's office knows we're coming so we don't get arrested."

"You think of everything." Shelby made a quick move and straddled him on the couch, then started lifting the hem of her shirt. "I love that about you."

That wife of his always had the best ideas. Getting naked was definitely a sound plan. He picked her up, carrying her toward the stairs while she went to work on his shirt buttons. "No, but I'll let you remind me of all the reasons you love me when we get upstairs."

"We're going to be up there for a long time," she said, wrapping those long legs of hers around his waist.

Damn. He'd be lucky to stay in control until they got to the bedroom the way this was going. Good thing Alex hadn't figured out how to break out of his crib yet.

"That sounds about as close to perfect as it can get to me."

And it was.

About the Author

Avery Flynn has three slightly wild children, loves a hockey-addicted husband, and is desperately hoping someone invents the coffee IV drip. Find out more about Avery on her website, follow her on Twitter, like her on her Facebook page, or friend her on her Facebook profile. Join her street team, The Flynnbots, on Facebook. Also, if you figure out how to send Oreos through the internet, she'll be your best friend for life.

Also by Avery Flynn…

BUTTERFACE

MUFFIN TOP

TOMBOY

THE NEGOTIATOR

THE CHARMER

THE SCHEMER

KILLER TEMPTATION

KILLER CHARM

KILLER ATTRACTION

KILLER SEDUCTION

BETTING ON THE BILLIONAIRE

ENEMIES ON TAP

DODGING TEMPTATION

HIS UNDERCOVER PRINCESS

HER ENEMY PROTECTOR

DADDY DILEMMA

PARENTAL GUIDANCE

AWK-WEIRD

LOUD MOUTH

WRONG BROTHER, BEST MAN

ROYAL BASTARD

THE WEDDING DATE DISASTER

Discover more Amara titles...

FAKE IT TILL YOU MAKE IT
an *Accidentally Viral* novel by Anne Harper

After accidentally making her secret blog public, everyone's dying to know who Sloane's never-got-over-him crush "Guy" is. She's even got a book deal offer—if she gets closure with "Guy." Too bad he's engaged. Brady Knox knows the truth. And he'll pretend to be "Guy" if Sloane uses her newfound fame to bring business to his bar. But keeping secrets in a small town isn't easy. And Brady wasn't meant to be anyone's perfect guy.

THE TWO-DATE RULE
a *Smokejumper* novel by Tawna Fenske

Willa Frank never goes on a date with anyone more than twice… until she meets Grady Billman. After their first date, Grady isn't ready to call it quits, so he finds a sneaky way around the two-date rule. And with every "non-date" Grady suggests, Willa must admit she's having fun playing along. But when their time together costs Willa two critical clients, it's clear she needs to focus on the only thing that matters—her future.

Hooked on You
a novel by Cathryn Fox

I'm not in small town Nova Scotia to hook up. I'm here to settle my grandmother's estate and sell the B&B, which I soon discover has been overrun with seasonal fisherman and operated on the honor system. The hard-core fishing folks become an instant family—the one I never had. Then there's the blind pet cow, who has a crush on my hot fisherman, Nate. Okay, technically he's not mine. I have no desire to get reeled in.

Matzah Ball Surprise
a novel by Laura Brown

Gaby Fineberg needs a date for Passover Seder, just for the weekend, and the hot guy at her gym would be perfect. But when she asks him, he doesn't hear a word she said. Levi Miller is deaf and happily single. He doesn't know Gaby, but it's clear she needs help with something—and suddenly so does he. Gaby pretends to be his new girlfriend to bail him out…and now he must return the favor.

Made in the USA
Coppell, TX
09 August 2020